The Twilight Howl

JK Brandon

ONE *Sometime after midnight...*

I woke up with an awful feeling something was wrong.

I raised my head off the living room carpet and stared through the darkness at the front door, then down the hall. I could hear Meatloaf snoring a few feet away, so he wasn't the problem. My nose sampled the room air, my ears strained for the reason I snapped on high alert.

Nothin'.

Probably just a bad dream. I exhaled, closed my eyes and went back to sleep.

Then it woke me up again.

This time I got up, quietly.

Robert—my master—hates it when we wake him up in the middle of the dark time for no good reason. I left my buddy Meatloaf plastered on the rug and padded to the back of the house. I looked out the big glass door at the backyard. The low lights were on around the patio, so I stood there and scanned for movement outside. There was a breeze comin' off the mountains and it moved small stuff around the yard. A tiny piece of paper blew by, then some dried tree leaves. It all seemed normal.

No cats.

No rabbits.

No coyotes.

Still, I had this bad feelin'. My stomach churned and a whine started in my throat. I swallowed it, not wantin' to wake my human.

I thought about goin' outside to look around, but it felt like the problem was inside our house, like maybe the kitchen. I went in there and sniffed around the floor for roach tracks.

Nothin'.

5

I sniffed the garbage pail under the sink but there was nothing unusual in there. An empty jar of spaghetti sauce—garlic with mushrooms. Lettuce leaves. Yecch. An empty wine bottle—red. Couple pieces of dry pasta—vermicelli.

It was just last night's dinner stuff in the plastic garbage bag, no problem with that. Except when Robert makes spaghetti for dinner, there's no leftovers for us to eat. Meatloaf thinks that's a big problem.

I wasn't sure what time it was, but it was pretty late, judging how quiet it was in the neighborhood. No cars drivin' by, no kids talkin' loud, no neighbor televisions on.

I kept lookin', I still had this sense of danger.

I knew the problem wasn't Robert walkin' around upstairs, we can always hear when he gets up. We hear the waterbowl flush, then he stumbles back to bed. It's not Robert. And since Judy left, there's no one else in the bedrooms upstairs.

Nobody misses Judy.

Now the lid on the big white waterbowl is up all the time.

I wandered over to the front door and stood there next to it with my head down, concentrating, listening. I didn't hear nothin', but I didn't expect to. The house across the street was empty, the old woman who lived there finally moved away. Me and Meat are plenty glad about that, all she did was complain about us barking at cats. You'd think she'd be grateful she had two sharp-eyed Black Labradors lookin' out for the neighborhood.

Better make that one sharp-eyed Lab. Meatloaf, he's more casual about things.

I went down the hall, then in the laundry room and stood there. The hairs on my coat stood up and my skin crawled. Somethin' didn't smell right. I picked up the usual stink of bleach and soap, sure. They were just strong smells coverin' everything else up. But something else was there, a faint smell I'd never nosed before. And this smell scared me.

"Woof."

It just popped out of my mouth.

"Woof."

Then another one snuck out.

Suddenly Meatloaf was standin' in the doorway, lookin' at me through sleepy eyes, head cocked in question. "What is it Taser?"

"I dunno," I said. "Somethin' doesn't smell right."

He put his nose up in the air and sniffed three or four times. "I don't smell anything weird," he said.

That didn't surprise me; my nose is legendary around the neighborhood. It's killer. Way back my in my Lab line there's some Bluetick Coonhound mixed in. My mother said it's why my ears are so big, but mostly it's why my sense of smell is so awesome.

"WOOF!" I barked even louder this time. "WOOF WOOF!"

Taser! Meatloaf! No barking!

It was Robert at the top of the stairs.

Go lay down.

I knew he wouldn't like the noise. He probably thought we were barking at stray critters in the yard.

"Thanks a lot, Taser." Meatloaf strolled back to his spot in the living room. "Come on, dawg. There's nothing wrong in there."

I followed him with my head hanging, then plopped down close by on the rug, still not happy about things.

I wasn't so sure nothing was wrong.

Not sure at all.

But I shut it.

For a while.

Then a whine leaked out.

Hennnng Hennnng Hennnng

"Zip it, dawg. Robert is gonna put us in the garage."

I jumped up and went back in the laundry room, the smell was worse. It smelled kinda like when Judy tried to make Sunday morning pancakes. Robert called them lawyer pancakes, whatever that is. They used to come out black on one side so she'd give them to us and we'd have to eat them. I usually gave mine to Meatloaf.

7

I walked around the room. The bad smell was comin' from one wall. I sniffed it good, stoppin' at the plug thing.

Pop!

Just then I saw sparks jump out of the wall socket and smelled smoke. I'm not sure why but I knew this was very bad.

"WOOF WOOF WOOF WOOF!"

Even Meatloaf started barking from his spot in the living room.

"BOW WOW! BOW WOW!"

We wouldn't let up. Pretty soon we saw Robert comin' down the stairs in his shorts. He came in the room and then turned around and ran into the garage. When he came back he had this big can with a hose and he squirted somethin' on the wall.

Then this awful noise started blarin'.

AAANNNNNGGGGGAAAANNNNNGGGG!!

I think it was the fire alarm. Robert went to the telephone and called somebody while Meatloaf and I barked like the house was on fire, and then I realized that it was.

"WOOF WOOF WOOF WOOF!"

"BOW WOW! BOW WOW!"

There was more smoke in the room, so we stayed away but kept barkin'.

Robert squirted some more stuff from the can, and then all of a sudden he ran out front and started draggin' the garden hose through the door. About then this long truck rolled up in front and these humans with rubber coats and funny hats ran in the house. They knocked holes in the wall and next there's water sprayin' and lights flashin' and siren's wailin'.

Awesome.

It was a lot of fun, but it got a little too-crazy, even for Labradors. The commotion started to scare us, so Meatloaf and I went out the dog door to the back yard and sat by the rear fence with our tail between our legs. We looked so pathetic I figured somebody would give us some pats and maybe a dog bone.

Robert came out and checked on us, and then he told us to stay, like we were gonna go somewhere more fun. Fat chance. We waited there until the big truck and the guys in funny hats left, then we went inside and stood with Robert.

It smelled like black lawyer pancakes all over the house. Water covered the floor and black soot smeared the walls in the hallway. I peeked in the laundry room, it looked like ten puppies had spent the week in there.

Robert got the mop and a bucket and got most of the water up, then he went in the kitchen and called to us.

Come on, guys.

He got a new box of dog biscuits off the pantry high shelf and started givin' us treats. Meat and I musta ate half the box, it was great. I don't know what we did to deserve it, but our stomachs were happy about it. We were thankful for the excitement too, because Labs need to have fun, even if it turned out to be trouble.

Little did we know, the fun was over and the trouble was just starting.

TWO *Wednesday Morning*

Trouble arrived the next morning with the big movinvan that pulled up across the street. Robert and I were outside getting the news papers when we saw it arrive.

We got this same routine every morning. First, Meatloaf and I wait at the foot of the stairs for Robert to come down. Then we squirm on the floor like brainless puppies until we get our bellies rubbed, then Robert and I go outside. He picks up the papers and I chase away any rabbits that think they can munch our Lantana flowers and get away with it. Then I pee on the bushes and we go back inside. Meanwhile, Meatloaf is waiting by his food bowl with hurry-up plastered all over his face.

But this morning when we got outside, Robert stopped to talk to the man who lived next door and that's when I heard the movinvan word. That's a new one to me, so I tried to figure it out. Then I saw humans taking furniture out the back of the truck and movin' it in the house.

That's how I learned so many human words, you just gotta pay attention when they talk. Humans may screw-up a lot of things, but they talk good because they got a better mouth than dogs. Human lips are in front of their head. Dog lips start on one side of our head and go all the way around to the other side. What's up with that?

Besides, half time my mouth is gotta hang open so I can pant, so what do you want from us?

When we got our food, Meat and I raced to scarf it down so we could steal what was left from the other's bowl. Meatloaf usually wins the food race, I suppose that's why he's kinda fat. He doesn't even chew it, he just sucks up the nuggets like that machine Robert uses to pickup all the dog hair on the floor.

After we ate first meal, we hung around the kitchen and watched Robert cook his breakfast. We stayed close by, because you never know if a piece of bacon is gonna fall from the sky and land near your nose.

Hey. It's happened.

Robert put his food on the table and ate while he reads the news papers. Pretty soon he starts grumblin'.

"What's he saying?" Meatloaf asked. "He's mad about something. Is he paying bills again?"

Robert always got mad when he paid the bills, he says there's never enough money. But he usually paid bills at night. In the morning he read the news.

I looked up at Robert, then back at Meatloaf.

"It's probably politics," I said.

Meatloaf knows I'm smarter than him, so he asks me the hard questions. It's not Meat's fault that he's a little slow, so I don't tease him about it. Meatloaf is a victim of second-hand marijuana smoke. It was from his first human, when he lived in Fresno in the country of California. Meat said it was medical marijuana, but I don't think it was good medicine for dogs.

"Politics," I said. "That's just people fighting."

"What are they fighting over?"

"Money. One side has all the money, the other side wants the money they have."

Meatloaf cocked his head. "Where does money come from?"

"Workin'. Like Robert does when he comes downstairs with his shiny shoes. That's a day when he goes off to Phoenix to work. When he's done workin', they give him money so he can buy our dog food."

"So working is good. Why don't we go with him and help? There might be more dog food around here."

"Dogs work at home," I said. "We chase away cats and guard the house. We give our humans love. Then they pay us with our chow."

Wham!

Robert slammed the paper down on the kitchen table and yelled Funk. Sometimes he calls for Funk when he's mad or hurts himself.

11

I'm not sure who Funk is, but he seems to be in demand. Meatloaf and I jumped at the loud noise and hugged the floor.

"Must be really bad politics today," Meatloaf said.

I listened closely to Robert mumblin' about it until I understood. "It's the govament and taxes. He's talkin' about them raising taxes some more."

Meat looked at me funny, so I explained. "That's the other way to get money—just take it. The govament takes taxes—

"Wait," Meatloaf said. "What's the govament?"

"They're like the dogcatcher for the whole world. But instead of taking away stray dogs, they take tax money away from people who work."

"But what if you don't work?"

"Then the govament doesn't take your money, they give you money."

Meatloaf looked confused.

I nodded. "I know, it's complicated. Nobody else can figure it out, either."

We stopped talkin' when a couple pieces of bacon fell on the floor in front of our nose. We opened our mouths and they were gone in one chomp. Bacon is not complicated.

Robert got up and moved dishes off the table while we watched closely, just in case there was any food still left on the plate he forgot to give us. He washed stuff in the sink and then headed for the garage. He came back inside with a wood doggie gate to keep us out of the laundry room area, and then he looked down at us.

I'll be back tonight.

I like it when he says that.

Normally, we watch television after Robert leaves. It's how we find out stuff and learn new words. I like the Animal Channel, my buddy likes the Food Channel. But today we had some new business to watch first.

We went to the front window and watched Robert drive away in his Jeep, and then checked the activity across the street. The movinvan humans were still takin' stuff inside the house.

"Looks like we're gettin' new neighbors for sure," I said.

Meatloaf stared at all the different people walking around the front of the house. "I think it's a woman moving in."

I tried to see myself. "You sure?"

"I think so."

"She's not old, is she?"

"Nope."

That was good. We didn't need any more complaints to the Homeowners Association. Robert said we were at our complaint limit with them. They got this really crabby guy over there, I don't think he likes dogs. Or barking, Or chewed plants in his yard.

I looked closer. Meat was right, a female was tellin' the other males where to move the furniture. That was normal, I thought.

Meatloaf seemed happy about it. "A new female-human across the street, that's great. Maybe her and Robert will mate."

"Yeah, maybe." I tried to judge how old she was, but I couldn't tell. "Doesn't she look kinda middle aged to you?" I said.

"No, only four or five."

"How old is Robert?"

"Five, maybe five and a half."

That was promising. He should like this female, she had the right look. I knew what male-humans liked, because you see those popular female-humans all the time on the television. She didn't have hair like a Golden Retriever, but she did have a chest like a Bulldog.

I looked closer. Maybe it was more like a small bulldog.

Catcrap. That might not work.

I pointed my nose at her. "You think her chest is big enough?"

Meat sighed. "I dunno dawg, we'll see what Robert does."

We knew male-humans acted like goofy puppies when they talk to females with a big chest.

Meat and I had been talkin' for days, and we thought Robert needed a new mate. Ever since Judy left, Robert seemed a little sad. He just hung around the house and didn't go out much. A guy can only watch so much television before he gets bored. Even with Bulldog chests on all the channels.

"What if we get another bad female?" Meatloaf asked.

That did worry me a little, but I wanted Robert to be happy. Lately he'd been walkin' around with a face like Bloodhound who'd lost his sense of smell. It's hard to be happy when your master is sad. When you're a Labrador, happy is important.

Besides, dogs gotta take care of their human so they can survive themselves. Even puppies figure that out early.

"I hope she's not another lawyer," I said.

"What are the chances of that?" Meatloaf asked.

"In Scottsdale, pretty good."

"Maybe this one won't make pancakes."

That was the least of my worries. I figured Robert was out of practice, that he wouldn't know how to find a mate. I thought I'd ask Meatloaf, he was a little older and had been with a lot of different dogs.

"Hey Meat, what's the secret to attracting females?"

Meatloaf scratched behind his ear. "No secret. Sniff around and see if they're in heat. Then just mount 'em."

I didn't think it worked that way with humans, and I told him so.

He agreed. "Yeah, because it's hard to tell if female-humans are in heat. But there's clues, even if you can't smell 'em."

I was doubtful, so I tested him. "What about the female across the street, is she in heat?"

Meatloaf looked out the window. "Nope."

"How can you be sure?" I asked

"Look at what she's wearing."

I looked across the street. All I could see was she had her clothes on. "So? She's all dressed."

"Are her clothes loose or tight?"

"Loose," I said.

"How about her shoes? What's she wearing?"

I looked at her feet. "She's wearin' those rubber shoes, the ones impossible to eat."

"Tennis shoes," Meatloaf said. "No female in heat wears sloppy clothes and tennis shoes. That's what they wear after they get the male-human to come live with them."

It sounded like Meat did know some female-human stuff after all.

He went on. "My last human was a female. When she was in heat, she'd wear tight clothes and ho-heels just before she went out at night."

"Ho-heels?" I'd never heard of those.

"That's what she called them. You know, those shoes taller than a Chihuahua that make females walk funny."

I knew before female-humans were complicated, but this was a lot of new information. Meat would probably still be with that same female, but she gave him away to Robert because one day he ate some of her underpants.

"Maybe we should ask Winston for his ideas tonight."

Winston was an English Bulldog who lived in our neighborhood. We usually saw him at the park after dinner. He was a little odd, but well informed.

"Good idea," Meatloaf said. "Winston knows a lot about human mounting."

Winston knew about almost everything. His humans were retired school teachers who spent a lot of time in front of the television. Winston picked up some great information and that was good, because we needed it around here.

I was looking forward to telling the dogs at the park about our house fire. Most of the time, it's awful boring in our neighborhood. The last excitement was when me and Meatloaf caught the murder-human down the street.

15

I made a memory to see what the dogs at the park thought about things.

THREE *Wednesday Night*

Robert came home after work carryin' this huge pizza box that smelled wonderful. We actually wanted the box more than the pizza, but food wasn't our main concern. Not mine anyway. I was getting' a little worried 'cause it was late and I didn't want to miss our walk to the park.

We wagged our butts like idiots when Robert came in the front door. It's embarrassing to hafta act that way at our age, but he expects it now and we didn't want to disappoint him.

I checked out his pant legs for any changes, but it all smelled normal. I'm not sure what he does at his Phoenix work, but it smells boring.

We got our normal dry dog food for second meal, weight control for Meat and high-performance for me. As soon as the bowls hit the floor the race was on.

Meatloaf and I are the same breed but two different types. Labradors are either English type or American type. The American Lab is tall and lanky, the English Lab is medium height and heavier. They're shorter and wider—like me. Meatloaf's a mix of the two, he's tall and he's heavy. I guess that's why he's always hungry.

We watched Robert eat the pizza until he was done, then he gave us a little piece. Then we watched some more, just in case.

He talked to us about his workstuff, and he asked if we'd been good dogs. I hate when they ask that, so I pretended not to understand. I figure he was gonna find that hole I dug in the backyard soon enough. I didn't feel bad about it, I needed that plastic sprinkler head more than that stupid plant did.

After everybody ate, Robert sat and stared at his computer screen. It didn't look like he was plannin' to take us to the park after all, so we used our favorite dog trick. We sat in front and stared at him, not sayin' a word, just starin', and after a while he gave up. It wasn't much

17

of a challenge. I think we could stare the paint off the wall if we wanted to. Finally, Robert opened the front door and we ran out. It was late, not really light and not really dark—twilight, I think they call it.

I checked the house across the street, but nothin' was shakin' so I took off for the park, Meatloaf limpin' along right behind. That's normal, the vet says he's got a touch of arthritis. It slows him down a little, nothin' serious.

The park is only a few houses away, so it feels like our private spot, but it really belongs to the whole neighborhood. We live in the Arizona desert, but our Scottsdale park is all grass. Behind the park is raw desert land, a preserve or something. It goes all the way up to the mountains. That's where the coyotes and the cactus and the scorpions and the snakes live. It's a scary place and we try to stay away.

When I got to the park, the first thing I did was pee about a gallon on a bush, then went sniffing to get the day's news. All the scents seemed familiar, but there was one special scent I hoped to catch. I hoped Simba might be there. I picked her up, but the scent wasn't fresh.

Simba's my main mount, a gorgeous Golden Retriever with great legs and serious dog breath. I looked far out in the park, but I didn't see her. I looked behind to where the humans were talkin' together in a group, but her owner wasn't there either. I was disappointed, but that's how it is. Sometimes you miss seeing the dogs that come early or late.

All of a sudden Gizmo ran up. Gizmo is a Jack Russell that can do amazing stuff. I've seen him bounce off walls like a tennis ball. He says he's a big dog trapped in a little dog's body, and I believe that. The pup's got attitude and the stuff to back it up.

"What happened at your house?" he asked. "I heard some sirens last night."

"The house caught fire. Taser saved us from burning to death," said Meatloaf. "He's a real hero."

"Meat, please." I told Gizmo the story, and then I told Roxie when she walked up. Roxie is a Fox Terrier and a really cool girl. She fits right in with the guys, you can lick your scrotum right in front of her, no problem.

"So the fire started in the wall?"

"That's what it smelled like. At first I didn't know what it was, then I saw sparks and white smoke."

"Bad wiring," said Gizmo. "You gotta be careful when it comes to those wires. My first human was an electrician. He knew all that stuff."

That kind of information was why I liked to come to the park, you learn stuff from dogs you can't find on television. I don't think the television people know very much.

Meatloaf jumped in. "I chewed through a lamp cord once. Wow! That's the last time I ever bit down on one of those. I peed all over myself."

Gizmo nodded. "You were lucky. Electric wires can kill you." Suddenly he called out to a new arrival. "Hey Winston."

We turned around and saw Winston waddling over. The squat English bulldog was wider than he was tall, with a flat nose that looked like he ran into the wall too-many times. But if that was true, it hadn't hurt his brain much. Winston was smart, he knows millions of human words. We think it's because his female human talks all the time and he picks it up.

"Have you all heard?" Winston asked us.

"About Taser's fire?" Gizmo asked. "He just told us about it."

Winston shook his head. "No, about the robbery. Two streets over. Some blaggard broke-in the house next to Spike and nicked the jewelry. That's the second robbery in a fortnight."

Spike was a dog we all knew in the neighborhood.

"I didn't even hear about the first robbery," I said.

"Me neither," said Roxie.

"What's a fort night?" Meatloaf asked.

19

Winston ignored him. "In the first pinch they nabbed a pocketbook full of cash. I'm tellin' you, this neighborhood's turned dodgy. All the upstanding blokes are leaving."

"I'll second that."

It was Remi, the miniature French Poodle with the weepy eyes. The fuzzy little dog turned my stomach. He used to be the best friend of my worst enemy, Bandit the weasely Weimaraner. Ever since Bandit moved away, Remi took over as the most obnoxious dog in our pack. He's always braggin' his master gives him canned dog food instead of dry nuggets.

Remi continued. "Now that housing prices are depressed, there seems to be a lower-class element moving in. The humans who come here now have automobiles so old they leak oil on the driveway!"

"No!"

"And they leave their garbage cans out on the curb for days."

"Disgusting."

"I thought this was a rich neighborhood," Roxie said, hanging her head. "Maybe we should move."

"A lot of people are moving away."

Gizmo raised a paw. "I counted empty houses yesterday when we were driving home from the store. There were at least ten, and a lot of them had dead lawns or broken windows."

"It's because of the increase in foreclosures," Remi said. "An unfortunate side effect of the ailing economy. If you were better informed, you'd know that. It's all over CNN television news."

Roxie coughed like she'd choked on a soup bone. "Come, on Remi. Nobody watches CNN anymore."

Meatloaf sighed. "I suppose I could go back to Fresno."

"Now wait, don't give up on our neighborhood," I said. "We just had someone move in across the street, a nice female. It will come back, I've seen this no-money time before."

"When?"

I thought a minute. "Two humans ago."

When I remembered what happened in the last no-money time, I got worried. I was dumped at the pound when there were four-closings and a bad economy.

Remi didn't help my worries with his next story.

"Well. I must tell you. I've heard dreadful stories about humans abandoning their dogs and moving away. They simply leave them in the yard and drive off."

"No!"

"Not our masters," I said.

"I wasn't talking about *my* master, of course," Remi said. "He understands I'm too valuable to simply discard."

"You're right," said Meatloaf. "He'll probably sell you to a Vietnamese restaurant."

Remi sniffed. "One might expect such comments from a creature with the name of, 'Meatloaf.'"

Meatloaf growled. "Oh yeah? How'd you like a piece of meatloaf, fuzzface."

I tried to head it off. "Wait, let's talk about something else. Like the fire."

Gizmo told Winston and Remi about the fire at our house.

"So," Winston said to me. "Your master probably wanted to burn the place down so he could get out from under the payments."

"Hey, hold on there," Meatloaf said.

Winston made me mad, too. I didn't like dogs talkin' trash about my master. It got me hot under my dog collar, but I let it go. "No, that's not it."

Winston kept it up. "Can't say as I blame Robert. What with Judy gone, it must be a bugger to make the payments."

It sounded like a good time to question him on mating. "We been wantin' to ask you about that, Winston. With Judy gone, we think Robert is lonely. We think he needs a new female. How do you get one of those?"

21

Winston puffed out his massive chest. "Personally, I never had a problem finding Bulldog dollies. But for humans, I think your Robert would be better-off if he kept the house. Human females want a stable home and a secure income. How are his finances?"

"His what?

"Does he have any money?"

I looked at Meatloaf and he shrugged.

"We don't know. We know he goes to work in Phoenix."

"He doesn't need money to attract females," Roxie said. "But it helps."

Meatloaf had a great idea. "Maybe Robert can get some money from the govament by not working."

"The government doesn't have any more money." Gizmo said. "They have to borrow all their money now from China."

All the dogs looked at Gizmo and cocked their head.

"The Bloomberg Channel," he said.

"Money's not absolutely necessary," Winston said. "Mostly, Robert needs to talk nice to the females. Be polite. He'll charm the skirt off one soon enough."

I pointed my nose down the street toward our house. "We were thinking about attracting the new female who moved in across the street. She looks like she could help make the payments."

"The problem is, we don't know if she's in heat," Meatloaf added. "Any ideas?"

"Well," Winston said. "First he needs to—

Suddenly Winston stopped talking and turned a floppy ear up to the sky. A weak moan floated through the park.

Ooooooooooooooooooooooooooooooo.

"What was that?" Gizmo asked.

"I didn't hear anything."

"Listen."

Ooooooooooooooooooooooooooooooo.

"I heard it this time."

It was a faint sound, a pitiful howl coming from somewhere faraway. We turned our heads toward the source and listened closely. Nobody barked. We waited and it came again.

Ooooooooooooooooooooooooooooooooo.

"It sounds like a call for help," I said.

"Nonsense," said Winston.

Meatloaf yawned. "Nah. It's just a dog wanting his second meal. Probably his owner is late getting home."

"No, listen," I said. "It sounds desperate."

We waited, but the howl didn't come again.

"It sounded familiar," Roxie said. "Who's not here?"

"Spike."

"Please," Remi said. "Spike lives two streets away. That's much closer than the source of that pathetic howl."

"Maybe it's Simba."

I shook my muzzle. "Not her. I know her sound."

"It almost sounded like Harley," Roxie said.

Harley was the Rottweiler who lived next door to us. He was a human biter, so he never got to go to the park, unless he snuck out. Which he did a lot, usually when their pool man left the gate open.

"No, it came from farther away," I said. "Maybe that subdivision across the big road, but definitely not from our neighborhood."

Roxie raised her voice. "It's Harley, I tell you."

Roxie had a thing for the big Rottweiler. Everybody knew that.

"Nonsense. Harley's probably sleeping at home."

All of a sudden we heard Robert call our names.

Taser! Meatloaf! Time to go.

We left the group and ran back to him, it looked like we'd have to finish this conversation another day. It was almost dark.

I let Meatloaf get ahead on the walk while I trailed behind. I wanted to watch Robert to see what he did.

Just like I thought, he turned his head and stared at the house across the street. I figured he must have seen the female's chest this morning and wanted to investigate further. But no one seemed to be home over there, the windows were dark and I didn't see any cars in front.

We went back in the house and drank a bowl of water the best we could. It took a while because you can only get a tongue's worth at a time, and then half of it leaks out the side of our mouth. At least our nose works great.

After drinking we watched the television with Robert. He didn't seem like he was lonely right then, but we wanted to make sure he was ok. We sprawled out in the little living room with the big television and panted and slobbered. We took up so much room, it looked like wall-to-wall Black Labradors for a while.

We're both big males, but the vet says I'm 85 pounds of muscle and Meatloaf was a hundred pounds of fat. He's lost some weight since the Vet yelled at Robert, but when he lays down his extra skin spreads out like spilt gravy. Not that spilt gravy's a bad thing.

Robert changed the floor stuff in this room to some tile with black streaks in it so you can't tell how much dog hair is here. We shed twice a year and it used to make Judy crazy, she was always cleaning up our hair with that push-motor machine while giving us dirty looks. It was probably why she left.

After some serious channel flippin', Robert finally put a movie on with a lot of loud explosions that made it hard to sleep. It didn't seem to bother Meatloaf's sleepin', so I got up and went outside by myself. I was still thinkin' about that howl we heard at another twilight, and it creeped me out a little. It was worrisome, but sometimes I think I worry too much. On the other paw, when you're the alpha dog for the neighborhood, you gotta take care of things.

Roxie had sworn it sounded like Harley, so I guess that's why I ended-up on his side of the yard. I figured I'd ask him since he lived right next door.

I went to our rear fence separating us from the desert. We have a metal slat fence, so you can look right out at the desert and see the cactus and the mountains. Harley had the same metal fence so we can

24

talk good, even if we can't see each other. It's kinda like bein' in the dog pound, somethin' I remember all too well. I stood in the corner and barked once for Harley.

Woof.

So I'm standin' there thinkin', and I realize I haven't heard Harley bark at us for a while. I'm not sure how long it's been, 'cause like most dogs, I live in the present moment, unless I'm rememberin' real hard. I thought it was weird we hadn't heard him, he used to bark every evening when we went out the door to the park. I always figured he was jealous.

I put my black nose through the bars and sniffed, it smelled faintly of his Rottweiler poop, but nothin' fresh.

Woof.

I let him have it again, but he didn't bark back. I figured he could be in the house, but knew he woulda come out to see me unless he was eatin' or somethin'. Harley can only go in the backyard on account of bitin' a kid human one time and getting' sued by the parents. He claims the kid hit him with a golf club, so I thought it was justifiable dog biting, but humans probably thought different. That's why they're human.

Then I thought maybe Harley coulda broke out of the backyard and run off, he was always sneakin' out the gate or the front door.

I stared out at the open desert and hoped he wasn't stuck out there with a broken leg or somethin'. I been out there alone and trust me, it's no place for mutts, even tough Rottweilers. But I reckoned the howl came from somewhere else, not out in the desert. I made a memory to investigate nextday when Robert went off to work. I planned to go upstairs, look down in Harley's yard and see what the deal was.

Yeah, I know, goin' upstairs is against the rules, but this mystery was startin' to make my brain hurt.

FOUR *Wednesday Night, after midnight*

It was late when two gaunt coyotes crept through the drainage pipe into the grassy park and stopped to listen. The neighborhood was quiet—dead quiet, even for the late hour. Only the weak light from the narrow moon gave the coyotes pause, for they preferred to hunt when it was darkest.

It was a desperate hunger that drove them into the human world. Rabbits were scarce in the wild, and the remaining desert rabbits were cunning and illusive, for they were desperate to live themselves.

Ikal and Seti were young coyotes, only one year had passed since they were born in their tiny den under a thick mesquite tree. At first they played and slept and ate what their mother brought to them, but soon they followed her further and further away on the hunt for food. They learned which trails and which sandwashes had game. They watched their mother catch small rodents and larger rabbits. When they were large enough, they caught the weaker rodents, when they were swift enough, they caught the faster rabbits.

But this night slow rabbits brought them into the park and the human world. Rabbits who lived by humans were awkward and overweight, like the dogs that barked at Ikal and Seti as they walked the streets. The two coyotes had no fear of these domestic creatures, these dogs were trapped in their human's house and weak from hand feeding.

Ikal led the way through the park and down the wide, hard street. They did not look for rabbits close by, for these rabbits had grown wary of the two predators. They walked deep into this strange world to where the hunting was fresh, even knowing they were surrounded by man. They did not worry.

They grew up close to the human houses and did not fear man. They had never known pain at the hands of humans. Their mother called

26

them foolish, she said men were dangerous, but Ikal and Seti did not see this themselves so they did not believe it. They would not bear the pangs of hunger as their mother did when hunting was bad. The two brothers would travel to where the hunting was good.

At the rare time when man appeared, they ignored him. But when lights flashed from man's machines, they sensed danger and hid. When the machine passed and the lights had gone they returned to their hunt.

They were far into this world when they picked up the scent of fresh rabbit.

They hunted their quarry in pairs, one would flush and one would catch. As they nosed and dug at bushes close to a dark house, a rabbit suddenly burst from its den.

They sprinted after him, claws digging in the soft yard but slipping and useless on the hard street. This rabbit eluded their grasp, but they trotted back and waited close to the den until another rabbit emerged from the same spot. This one ran straight into Seti's quick mouth.

The plump rabbit perished in the crush of powerful jaws. Seti carried it away, then they crouched and shared the catch. They were almost finished eating when they heard a human machine and saw its lights at the next house. They stayed low to the ground, unwilling to leave their meal.

The machine stopped and two humans appeared, and then deep barking came from inside the house. The barking grew fiercer as doors slammed. Then the dog yelped once and was silent. Ikal heard a raised human voice, rough and forceful.

Ikal and Seti looked at each other but said nothing. They knew the voice of this barking dog, they had heard it speak before, but not at this house. They quickly finished their rabbit and jogged off into the night, hunger satisfied.

Each had a similar understanding of this night. They would stay away from this house and its men on future hunts.

FIVE *Thursday Morning*

The next day started like usual, but when we picked up the news papers this time we saw the new female neighbor across the street in her driveway. She waved at Robert and we both went over to talk to her.

She acted friendly and seemed happy, smiling with a nice face. She bent down and made this fuss over me, which I liked because not every female human was dog person. I checked her clothes out for drycleaner smells, but picked up only soap. That didn't smell like lawyer clothes to me.

Robert acted real polite and nice like Winston said he should, so I hoped there was a chance of some mating yet. They talked for a while, I didn't listen too close in case it was personal. But I picked up a few words.

Shannon…...Friendly….neighborhood….moved…...renting…California…...weat her

They never said anythin' interesting, except her name and the California part. The conversation didn't last too long, Robert said goodbye and then we went back in our house and ate first meal. Later, I filled Meatloaf in on the new female and Robert talkin'.

"Shannon," Meatloaf said. "Nice name. She buying or renting?"

"I heard the renting word. Is that bad?"

"It's temporary. You don't stay very long in a house if you rent it."

I wanted her to stay, so maybe that was bad. "Maybe she could rent half of this house from Robert. Winston said Robert had trouble makin' payments for the house since Judy left."

"They gotta mate first. Then he gets her rent money."

"We'll have to work on that."

"I like that she's from California," Meatloaf said. "Was it Northern California or Southern California?"

"How can you tell?" I asked.

"You can smell it. Even with my nose."

Meatloaf's nose didn't work very good, he said it because of all the second-hand marijuana smoke when he lived in Fresno.

I scratched a rib and thought about that. "That sounds like puppy-thinking, how can you smell where people came from?"

"Did you smell any silicone?"

"What's silicone?"

"Plastic, gushy plastic stuff. If they're from Southern California, they put it in their chest. You know, in those two lumps."

I thought. "I didn't smell anything like plastic."

"So she's from Northern California," Meat said.

"What do they do there?"

"Yoga. Like on that video Judy had. That's where I perfected my downward dog pose," he said.

Robert was ready to leave, so we walked him to the door. When I was sure he was gone, I ran to the stairs and started up. Meatloaf didn't like me goin' upstairs so he barked angrily at me.

"Taser! Don't do it, things have been going good for us lately."

"Sorry Meat. I gotta check this out." Meatloaf was mad at me for breakin' the rules,—No going upstairs and chewin' personal stuff.

So I disobeyed, no big deal.

I'm not a bad-dog, but sometimes I do bad things.

I moved carefully through Robert's bedroom so I didn't leave any evidence in there. I shoulda stayed out of there, but as long as I was upstairs I wanted to check it out.

It looked different than when Judy lived there. Robert had taken down the flowered wallpaper and painted it gray or somethin', but it was definitely more male human. And the flower-covered bed blanket was gone. Now he had black bed covers.

I went in his bedroom bathroom and saw his counter was still a mess. I sniffed. Male perfume. Stinky male-clothes. Mold in the water-shower. Wet towels. That was all normal, so I left it.

I padded over to the little bedroom where he worked on his model airplanes. He's got a window in there that looks down on Harley's house and into his backyard. The window shade was in the way, so I put my head underneath, moved it up and looked out the window.

I didn't see Harley anywhere. I looked closer but I didn't see any poop in the backyard, either. Yeah, it was probably too far away to trust dog's eyes, but it's not hard to find a pile from a Rottweiler as big as Harley.

It looked bad. I thought maybe they sold him, or sent him to the pound. There's a limit on what you can do bad, we all know that.

Then I saw the birds eatin' what was left of Harley's food in his bowl. That was enough to convince me. No dog still breathin' lets birds eat their food. I had to face the truth, it looked like our neighbor pal was gone.

I went downstairs and told Meatloaf what I'd found.

He shook his head. "That's tough. Roxie's gonna be real upset. Ever since he broke out that one time and slipped her the pinkie, she's stupid for him."

"I know. This is a tragedy."

He looked at me funny. "What's a tragedy?"

"The fact that Harley's missin'."

"No, dawg. What's that word, tragedy?"

"It's somethin' real bad."

"Why didn't you just say real bad?"

"Sorry, Meat. I been watching too much public television lately."

I gotta remember not to use big words in front of Meatloaf, he's sensitive about his brain. It's not quite a cat brain, but it's slower than your average canine.

"Look," Meatloaf said. "Dogs come, dogs go. Maybe his owner got tired of Harley breaking out and gave him away."

"No way," I said.

"Maybe he bit another person. Rule #3, two bites and you're out."

"But our neighbor loved that dog."

Meatloaf hesitated. "I hate to bring this up, but maybe Harley died. Maybe he got out and was run over by a car."

"Think so?"

He shrugged. "Catcrap happens."

I couldn't accept that, but Meatloaf had a different take on life, he was low-key about everything. His favorite thing was sleepin' in the sun out on the grass.

I tried to make my case. "What about that howl we heard last night?"

Meatloaf snorted like he had a wild hair up his nose. "Come on, that wasn't Harley. Harley's a tough old dog, he's mean."

"I dunno, it could have been him." I had to admit, I wasn't sure. Harley seemed tougher than the howl sounded.

"Taser, give it a rest. You're just looking for a problem to solve."

"I gotta take care of things, Meat. This could be serious. What if he's in trouble?"

Meatloaf plopped down on the tile and stretched out. "This is just your Labrador need for sick excitement. Chill out. I'll give you some of my seed pod stash from last year."

Meatloaf eats the seed pods that fall from our Mesquite tree in the hot time. He says they mellow him out. That's fine for him, but I don't like mellow.

I shook my head. "No thanks. I gotta stay sharp."

You never know when an emergency might arrive. I mean, somethin' like the house catchin' on fire.

I left Meatloaf to sleep while I went to watch some television. I stepped on the TV changer so I could see what was showin' on the big screen. I flipped around, then stopped at somethin' that looked promising for Robert. It was called 'The Bachelor,' or something like that. It was a male and a female human, and it looked like they wanted to be mates, or at least get mounted, 'cause they were sittin' real close and touchin' bodies.

They didn't smell each other, because humans don't do that before they mate. Humans hold hands and stare at each other's noses. That's how I knew this was an important show. I watched a while until I got bored. I left the TV on that channel so Robert could learn somethin' about mates.

After that, I got sleepy and joined my buddy sleepin' on the carpet. Even I gotta sleep during the day. Besides, I wanted to save my energy for the park.

***

When we heard Robert's Jeep pull in the garage, we ran to meet him. It felt like his normal time to be coming home, so that was good. Our evening priority is food and then the park. We got our priorities right, it's humans that screw them up.

Robert made eggs for dinner, but he didn't make any bacon. I think bacon's a first-meal thing. It smelled like he added some cheese and tomatoes and onions, none of which Meat or I had any interest in. I mean, we like scrambled eggs, but not with that other junk in them. He usually makes that when there's nothin' else good to eat.

He had a beer with his dinner, there's no mistaking that smell. Yecch. If some beer spills on the floor, Meatloaf will lick it up, but I won't touch it.

We sprawled on the floor so he had to step over us to move around the room. We like to be close to him, plus we don't want him to forget about us.

My German Shepherd friend from the pound used to say it took a long time for dogs to figure out how to survive. Major said we used to be wolves, then one time some of us came out of the forest to a human campfire and ate some of their food. After that, we stayed with them. Dominga said we got weak when we came to live with humans.

Dominga is a coyote I know from out in the desert. She doesn't like humans, but one time she did need to eat some human food I gave her to survive. Humans are not so bad, it's just that they do dumb things. That's why dogs gotta help 'em.

Personally, I'm happy with the setup we got here. We get two meals, doggie treats, a bone now and then, lots of love from our master, and dog pals in the neighborhood. I've been in worse homes, trust me, so has Meatloaf.

That's why I worried before about our neighbor dog, Harley. I knew it can be a lot tougher on a mutt than livin' in a house in this nice neighborhood. Masters can be mean or forget to feed you. But not around here. As far as Harley, it seemed like he was dead or long-gone. I tried to put him out of my brain.

When it got time for the park, Robert was on time, it was still light out. We ran ahead of him down the street to the park.

My Golden Retriever gal, Simba was already there, so I went right over to her. She smelled like she'd just got a bath. She gave me a little nip, then panted in my face so I could smell her dog breath.

"Hi Taser," she said.

"Hi doll. You smell great tonight."

"Liver treats," she said.

Her soft pink tongue panted in and out over her sharp white teeth. I checked out her soft, shiny coat and her long, strong thighs. She watched my eyes wander as she slowly switched her tail.

"See anything you like?" she teased.

Plenty, from where I stood.

She stood there panting like she wanted me to mount her, and for a minute I considered it, but I saw her female human was close by and figured she wouldn't like it. Female owners don't like when you hump their dog. Male owners, they don't seem to mind.

I know this because one time when I was on top of this hot little Lab-mix on the Westside, and her female human came out of the house screamin' like I was killing her dog. When she couldn't get me off she squirted me with a water hose. Can you believe that?

It was embarrassing.

Rude, too.

Gizmo was chasin' Roxie out in the park, so Simba and I took off to catch them. We chased each other for a long time, until we got hot and tired. It wasn't the hot time yet, but the cold time had passed, so there were lots of new leaves on the trees and lots of new flowers. That also meant there were lots of new rabbits, somethin' I wasn't too happy about.

We chased the ones we saw, but rabbits got these secret places to hide in the ground. What kind of self-respectin' creature lives in a hole in the ground?

Someday I'm gonna catch one of those long-eared rats.

When we had our fill of exercise, Simba, Gizmo, Roxie, and me ran back by our owners and stood, panting like we didn't have any sweat glands. Meatloaf was waitin' there, talkin' seriously with Winston about somethin'. That's how it is with Winston, he talks like a teacher in an dog-obedience class.

"Low cut dresses," Winston was saying. "If she comes over for dinner with a lot of bare chest showing, she's hoping for a little rumpy-pumpy."

"I beg your pardon?" Simba asked.

"Oh, sorry," Winston said. "I was just giving Meatloaf some tips on finding female-humans in heat."

"Robert's lonely," I explained quickly. "We want to mate him with the new female across the street."

"A new neighbor? I haven't smelled her yet," Simba said.

"What about ho-heels?" Meatloaf asked. "The shoes they wear just before mounting."

Simba looked right at me and cocked her head. She doesn't like it when the male dogs talk about mountin'.

I looked the other way and pretended I didn't hear what he said.

"Those tall shoes with the sharp heel?" Winston asked. "Another good sign. Especially with black stockings."

"Ok, sounds like it's time for me to go," Simba said.

34

"Wait, not yet." I had a theory, but it was almost too late to prove it. It was nearly dark outside and almost time for us to go.

I hoped Robert didn't want to leave. I looked over and he was still talkin' a lot, so I figured it would be a while, even if it was late.

Then we heard it, driftin' over on the still air.

Oooooooooooooooooooooooooooooooo.

"What was that?" Simba asked.

"It's Harley," Roxie said. "I'm positive now."

"Nonsense," Winston said. "It's a smaller dog."

"I'm not so sure."

Oooooooooooooooooooooooooooooooo.

Simba looked scared. "It sounds awful."

"It's a dog in trouble, that's for certain," I said. "Listen to that sad voice."

"We should help it. Maybe it's lost."

Oooooooooooooooooooooooooooooooo.

"Where's it coming from?" Gizmo asked, looking around.

We strained to pick up the direction of the cry, but it swirled around the park, seeming to come from everywhere. I thought it was bouncing off the mountains.

"Behind us. That howl is coming from our neighborhood."

Gizmo shook his head. "You're wrong, it's much further away."

"Come on, it's right over there behind the park."

Oooooooooooooooooooooooooooooooo.

I shivered at the sound.

We waited—then, just silence.

"Well that's it," Winston said finally. "The twilight howl."

"We gotta do something," Gizmo said. "It *is* a dog in trouble, big trouble."

Meatloaf spoke up. "Even if it is, there's nothing we can do, we're only dogs."

"Yeah, we're only dogs, but dogs gotta help each other," I said.

"No." Winston pawed the grass in protest. "Meatloaf is right. It's a dog-eat-dog world. Our obligation is to our humans, not other dogs."

Roxie hung her head. "I think Harley needs us. I can feel it now."

"You're guessing. That's not his howl."

"It could be Harley," I said. "I looked in his yard today, he's gone and he's been gone a while. It's possible he's out in the desert, maybe his leg is broken."

"Wait," Winston said. "This is new information. I didn't know Harley was missing from his backyard. Maybe he's caught in a trap out there."

"A trap?"

"A coyote trap. Some humans put coyote traps in the desert. They're made of steel and the jaws snap-closed on their leg when they step on it."

"That's awful," Simba said.

"It gets worse. When humans check the trap later, they kill the animal with a club on the head. Then they skin them and hang their coat on the wall."

Gizmo scoffed. "Come on, Winston. You're making that up."

"Hey. Put a sock in it, Gizmo. I only make-up stories about dollies. It's called trapping, I saw it on the Sportsman Channel. It's on everyday, right after my morning walk."

"Traps don't sound very sportsman like to me."

Meatloaf jumped in. "I bet Harley's dead. I bet he got out of his back yard and was hit by a car."

"Meat! You don't know that. You're gonna get Roxie all upset."

Roxie walked in a little circle and whined. Hennnngg. Hennnngg. Hennnngg.

"I'm sorry Roxie," Meatloaf said.

I raised a paw. "Roxie, let me think about this, there must be something we can do."

"Let's start with canine reconnaissance." Winston said. "I walk the neighborhood every morning with my humans. I'll search the streets for clues tomorrow."

"That's good, Winston." I didn't want to discourage his help, but I didn't think he could find anything around here. We had to get closer to the source.

Gizmo had a better idea. "We need to triangulate the howl. We need to get a fix on the location."

"What's triangulate?" Meatloaf asked.

Gizmo explained. "Our houses are all over the neighborhood. When we go home, listen closely for another howl. Remember what direction it comes from, and then we can compare them tomorrow night at the park. It should pinpoint the location."

"What if he doesn't howl again?" Roxie asked.

"Why would it only be one time? Why only now?"

I thought I knew. "Because the howl is meant for our ears. If it really is Harley, he would know that we're all together at the park at twilight time. He's calling to us for help."

Now it really bothered me, it sounded like a desperate situation.

"Taser's spot-on," Winston said. "The poor bloke is begging for our help."

"Taser," Gizmo said. "It's time for a road trip. We need to break out of our yards. We need to get closer and look for ourselves."

Meatloaf didn't like that idea. "No way. I'm tired of getting in trouble because you dawgs disobey."

I kept quiet, but I knew Gizmo was right, so I told the pack. "Let's listen tonight and see what happens. If we can locate the source it will save a lot of time. Until then, let's hope our friend is ok."

***

When we got home, Meatloaf and Robert watched television. I went outside and checked my doghouse for snakes or scorpions, but it

37

smelled all normal. I don't sleep in there a lot, but I'm glad to have it. You never know when it might come in handy.

I lay down on the patio, crossed my front paws and listened closely for the howl. I thought Gizmo's idea about finding the source was a good one. I sat there with my ears up, listening for another howl. Pretty soon my head started droopin' and I put it on my paws. Maybe I slept, maybe I didn't.

I don't know how long I was there, but the next thing I knew Meatloaf was outside on the patio. When I looked up he was looking down at me.

"Hey dawg, what are you doing, it's really late. Robert already went upstairs to bed."

My head snapped up. "I'm listening for Harley's howl," I said.

"Harley's dead."

I yawned. "You don't know that."

"You watch. There's gonna be a new puppy next door in a few days, then you'll know I'm right. Humans act all sad when their dog dies, then a little while later they show up with a new puppy and they forget all about the dead dog. It's kinda like when they get a new car 'cause the old one breaks down."

"Maybe. But 'til then we gotta try to find Harley."

"*You* can try if you need to. I don't have to prove anything."

I thought about that as a breeze started blowin', bringin' a bunch of new smells off the desert. The strongest smell was the creosote bush, it almost crowded out the rest. But then I got a faint whiff of animal, the kind that never got a bath—a wild animal. Smellin' it made me think of our old coyote friend.

"Do you ever think about Dominga?" I asked Meatloaf.

"Once in a while,' he said.

"I wonder if she's still out there."

"Probably. I bet the coyotes haven't moved that far away."

As long as the rains come, they stay away from our houses because they have enough food out there. But not always. Every now and then we hear reports of a coyote in the neighborhood. Sometimes you see one walkin' down the street in the early morning, but mostly it's the bloody remains of a cat in someone's backyard or a chewed rabbit in a yard. It don't bother me any, but it makes the little dogs nervous.

I spoke my thoughts out loud. "Maybe Dominga heard the twilight howl."

"Why do you care what she thinks?"

"I bet she'd know where it came from. I bet she could pinpoint the source. Coyotes are good hunters. What do we know about finding animals? All we can find is our dog dish."

Meatloaf raised his voice. "Ok dawg, I know what you're planning, so don't do it."

"I'm just thinking."

"Yeah." Meatloaf turned around to go back in the house. "First you think. Then you do something stupid."

That Meatloaf, always jokin' around.

I took in my last whiff of the night air and went inside, still thinking.

SIX *Friday Morning*

After Robert went to work, Meatloaf and I did our usual morning routine of sleepin' and watchin' television. It was gettin' harder to learn interesting new stuff, because of all the politics talk on all the channels. All I could find was television heads talkin'. I knew it was about politics because all the humans were ugly. The ugly humans only get to put their face on the television when the talk is politics.

All of a sudden the day turned crazy when Gizmo invaded our backyard.

"Wakeup!" he yelled. His bark blared throughout the house.

I got up to look, and I saw half a Jack Russell stuck through our dog door. "Gizmo you dawg, what's happening?"

He panted. "Got any water?"

"Come on in."

He ran to our bowl and drank sloppily, but he didn't drip back nearly as much on the floor as Meatloaf and I.

"My female human is out shopping," he said. "So I snuck out the side gate."

Gizmo could jump up and flip the gate latch. I'd done it a couple times myself, but he could jump much better than me. Like a kangaroo, he claimed. Whatever that is.

"Wanna do some investigating?"

"Sure do," I said.

"Not me." Meatloaf shook his head. "If I'm going to get in trouble, it will be for pulling a loaf of that white bread off the second pantry shelf."

That's my buddy.

"Let's go, Gizmo."

He and I went out the dog door to the side yard and he flipped the gate latch. It was no problem for him. I swear I've seen him jump five-feet straight up. Gizmo's got chest and leg muscles like those beefy guys on the Wrestling Channel.

We hustled out front.

"Where to?" I asked him.

He walked quickly to the house next door to us. "Let's check out Harley's place. Maybe we can find something." He stopped at the gate. You think anyone's home?"

I looked out front, all the cars were gone. "Nope."

Gizmo launched himself against the house, hit the wall and bounced to the top of the fence. He balanced there a minute, then jumped down. In a second Harley's gate was open and we were in the back yard walkin' around. Harley's yard was mostly grass with a few bushes, not like our yard. They did have a couple desert trees for shade, and I could see that's where Harley spent a lot of time.

"Check this, no dog poop," Gizmo noticed. "There ain't been a mutt back here for a while."

We walked around to the back patio. I spotted a chew toy layin' there all alone that I knew Harley loved. "That's Harley's favorite, he wouldn't have left it."

His water dish was turned over and his food dish was empty.

"It looks bad," Gizmo said.

I walked up to their glass door and looked inside the house. It was dark and deserted.

"Have they moved away?" Gizmo asked.

"No, I saw the male-human yesterday. He's a doctor and he works a lot. Sometimes Robert feeds Harley when he goes on vacation."

"Is there a female?"

"Once in a while, not all the time."

"Maybe the doctor took Harley with him on vacation."

"No way. Harley's a human biter."

"He says it was a bad rap, he really doesn't bite. He claims self-defense."

"That's what they all say."

41

We stood there, unsure of what to do next, just sure that Harley was gone. Then I had a thought. "Let's walk the neighborhood. Spike's only two streets over. Maybe he's heard the twilight howl and knows what direction it comes from."

"I like it."

Once we got outside Harley's gate, I put my butt against it and pushed until it latched. Then we took off on a half-run toward Spike's. We passed a couple cars drivin' down the street, but they didn't even look at us. We were careful crossin' the street 'cause I'd seen more than one dog squashed by a car when I lived on the Westside. It looked like a rough way to go. I'd seen my share of dried-out squashed cats, too. Frisbee-cats, we used to call em.

Gizmo paused at a street corner. "Is this his street?"

I sniffed the air and got a slight hit of garlic. "Yep." Spike's human was an old Italian guy from back east somewhere. Winston says he's a retired mafia hitman who's hiding in Arizona under witness protection. Spike won't confirm that, but he won't deny it either.

We took off on a run. Four houses later we found Spike in his usual spot, relaxin' on the front yard grass, tethered by a long rope tied to a tree. There was a water dish and a chew bone with him there in the shade.

Spike swung his head to look at us, his pointy Doberman ears tilted down in our direction. He seemed surprised to see us.

"What's dis? It's Blackie and his little buddy—Grimy, right?"

Gizmo flexed his chest muscles to look tough. "Name's Gizmo."

Spike looked down the street. "Where's Meatball?"

I looked at Gizmo. "He means Meatloaf." I looked back at Spike. "Sleepin', probably."

"Is dis a social call or are you comin' by to bust my chops for barkin' at cats?"

"Cats? Bark all you want," I said. "We wanted to know if you've heard that howl, the one that comes just before dark."

The Doberman looked down his long black snout at me. "Maybe I heard it and maybe I didn't. Whatzit too ya?"

"We think it's Harley, my neighbor. He's disappeared from his back yard. We been at the park last couple nights and heard it right at twilight," I said.

Gizmo jumped in. "We think he's calling to us for help."

"Dat right."

Spike didn't look concerned. He never cared much for our pack of dogs. He was a loner, just like his master. They hardly ever left their house, and when they went for a walk, they rarely came by the park. I couldn't remember the last time he'd been by to see us.

"A missin' pooch. Sounds like a mystery to me." Spike looked at me through narrowed eyes. "Still playin' deputy dog, I see. Stickin' your muzzle in other people's business."

He didn't care much for me, but I didn't let it bother me. "Hey. I'm just lookin' out for my friends. I'd do the same for you."

"I ain't your friend and I don't need no help."

"Fine, but what about Harley? He's a good dog."

"Dat's true, I always liked da big mutt. Rottweiler dat size, he'd be good to have on your side in a fight." He waited a minute then spoke. "Yeah, I heard the howl. Heard it twice in two days, same time. Sounded like Harley to me."

Gizmo's eyes got as round as food bowls. "Really? What direction did it come from?"

Spike jerked his head back. "Dose houses over by da big apartments. Back of da food store."

I knew the area he was talkin' about, it wasn't that far away. That part of our neighborhood was run down and older. "Are you sure?"

"Do I look like a joker to you? I told ya da truth. Besides, it's da direction he was walkin'."

Now I was confused. "You saw him walking by?"

"Somethin' wrong wit your ears, deputy dog? Yeah, I saw him walkin' dat way. Musta been last week some time."

This was great news.

"He walked by wittout sayin' a word. Looked like a dog on a mission. I figured he was on the move because he smelled some bitch in heat."

"Didn't you think that was weird?" Gizmo asked. "I mean, dogs are supposed to be on a leash in Scottsdale. It's the law."

Spike snorted. "Da law? Whadda cops gonna do, write a mutt a ticket? Big deal. I eat parkin' tickets for lunch. Cops don't scare me, and I doubt Harley gives a wit."

"Where do you think he went?"

"How should I know? I mind my own business. You should try it yourself, Blackie."

I was about to tell him I couldn't do that, but I didn't think he cared about that either. I was just happy to have some confirmation. "I guess we better get back, good to see you again, Spike."

"Likewise. Give my regards to Meatball." Spike moved to the center of his yard and lay down.

We walked back toward my house, both of us excited by the unexpected news. Gizmo walked so fast his muscular little legs were a blur. I had half-run to keep up.

He talked just as fast. "Where was Harley going?"

I didn't know, but I doubted he was looking for a female. "Maybe he was lookin' for his master. Maybe his human walked that way and he followed the scent."

"I don't know, Harley always seemed more interested in finding female dogs."

That was true, actually. He was pretty independent. His human filled his bowl once a day and he ate whenever he felt like it.

"This is what I think," Gizmo said. "It's all part of the weird things happening in the neighborhood. We've had robberies, vandalism, humans abandoning their houses and their dogs, and now dogs are wandering off and disappearing. It's almost like the neighborhood has curse on it."

"What's a curse?"

"It's a bad word, like funk."

"Funk. Who is that guy anyway? Robert is always calling him."

"We need the neighborhood cleaned up. We need more good people, more good dogs."

"Great, how do we get that?"

"I dunno. Maybe the pack will have some ideas tonight."

Our street was still deserted when we got to my house. It seemed like everybody who had a house had to work all day. That was probably why we all ended up at the park together after dinner. It's that money thing, again. I made a memory to check money out. It seemed like it was threatening our little world again.

Gizmo left me at the gate and ran home to get in before his female came home.

When I got inside, I filled Meatloaf in on our findings. He was interested, but said he was glad he stayed home.

"Look," Meatloaf said. "Don't get the idea I don't care about Harley, because I do. But all this runnin' around makes me tired. I want to get involved when you figure it out. I'm just not much for leg work. You're the one with all the energy."

I thought that was fair. Meat was most valuable when I had to run an idea by him to get his advice.

I teased him a little. "I know, you want to swoop in at the last minute and solve the mystery."

"Hey. Don't think I can't."

"Ok Meat."

He stretched out while I went in the other room to do some money research on the television screen. I put on the CNN Business Channel because I wanted to learn about the economy, which is the human word for not having enough money. I wanted to know why sometimes there was jobs and homes for dogs, and sometimes there wasn't any. If there was any way I could get money for Robert I wanted to help.

I must have watched television for most all of the day, and at the end I figured I knew as much as anyone did about the economy, which was nothin'. I mean, if they knew so much, why did it break so often?

And what's up with this stocks market stuff? After watchin' CNN Business and the Bloomberg Channel, I had it figured out. Apparently, in the New York country there's this famous street with a tall wall down the middle of it. On one side they keep bears and on the other side they keep bulls. It's a zoo, but with only two kinds of animals.

Anyway, all these guys in goofy coats stand around the wall and yell at each other, buying and selling pieces of paper that may be worthless or may be worth a lot of money, but nobody really knows for sure. Sometimes they buy too-many papers and sometimes they sell too-many papers, and that's when there's no jobs or homes for dogs.

Then, after screwin' everything up, these humans are all stressed-out, so they go to bars and drink lots of beer. That's pretty much it.

Needless to say, by the time Robert got home, I was ready for the park.

We had to wait on Robert while he made dinner and then stared at his little computer screen, but finally he got with the program and took us out the door. We had to run down the street to burn off our own stress, because they don't give dogs beer.

When we got there I saw Simba talkin' to a pooch I'd never seen before. I figured it was some visitor to our neighborhood. It was a male Chocolate Lab, he looked about four years old. He was a little bigger and a little taller than me. He had some decent muscle, but I didn't see any scars on him. I went over to sniff him out.

Eukanuba dry nuggets. Active Dog. Milkbone Doggie Treats.

Then I asked Simba. "Who's the stray?"

The new dog didn't seem to like that I interrupted his conversation with Simba, because he glared at me like I'd taken away his half-eaten food bowl.

Simba nodded in his direction. "This is Ranger. He just moved in the neighborhood." She pointed at me with her muzzle. "Ranger, this is Taser."

He cocked his head. "Taper?"

"No, Taser. Somethin' wrong with your ears?" I was a little irritated because he was a little-too familiar with my girl.

He came over and sniffed my butt. That's another thing that ticks me off.

That's two.

"What's this?" he asked. "A Black Lab? Like I've never smelled one of those before. Borrring. No offense, but if you've smelled one Black Lab, you've smelled them all."

Then he walked back to Simba. "But you, miss gorgeous Golden Retriever, you're one of a kind. Best of Show."

She panted in his face.

Ok. We had a problem here.

So I started out rude. I didn't want to go right to biting. "Pleased to meet you too, brownie," I said. "But what happened to your coat? Too much time in the sun? Your hair looks all bleached out."

He hacked like a cat with a hairball. "I'll have you know I'm a pure-bred."

A pure-bred weasel, I thought. "Pure-bred. You mean your parents had brown hair, too."

"No, I'm a registered, pure-bred Chocolate Labrador."

Oh brother. One of those.

"Wow!" I jumped up and down like I'd just met the President's dog. "You mean with official papers and shiny trophies and pretty ribbons and everything?"

Simba rolled her eyes.

"Well, no," Ranger said. "I lost my papers when I lost my humans. I'm a rescue Lab."

I looked him over. "Hard to believe someone would get rid of somethin' as valuable as you. But, lotta that goin' around. What with the funny stock papers market and bad economy and all."

He cocked his head. "Who cares about the economy as long as we get our food.?"

I wasn't about to tell him what I found out, so I just gave him the Taser stare. Simba saw it and tried to make peace. "Taser knows all that stuff because he watches television with his human."

Ranger sniffed. "Television. You mean the idiot box? My human reads books."

That was three. The new guy was really gettin' under my skin. "Hey. I'll catch ya later, dawgs."

I left Simba and Ranger and ran out in the park to run with the other pooches. I had to kill my anger or I was gonna bite the miserable cur. I really wanted to. So I ran after Gizmo to blow-off steam.

I hafta admit, Gizmo can run faster than me. His owner was there, he was throwin' a tennis ball for us to chase and return. We did this a while until we got tired. I was runnin' after my last ball when all of a sudden this brown flash goes by and plucks the ball away from my open jaws.

It was Ranger. After he stole the tennis ball, he didn't return it to be thrown again, he kept it and pranced around with it in his mouth. I looked over at Gizmo and he shrugged. Finally Ranger dropped our ball and started dancin'.

"Who's the dog!" Ranger crowed, over and over. "Who's the dog!"

Gizmo looked over at me. "Yeah. Who is that dog?"

"His name's Ranger. He just moved here." We left him and ran over to talk to the dog pack, but Ranger followed right behind us.

When we got there, Meatloaf was talkin' to Winston. "Nope, I never had a Pekinese, they're too short for me."

Winston was about to speak when the mystery howl floated in. I'd almost forgot about it in all the excitement of the new dog showin' up.

Ooooooooooooooooooooooooooooooooo.

"What's that?" Ranger asked.

Winston looked at Ranger. "Who are you?"

I told Winston and the pack about the new mutt, and then Gizmo asked everyone a question.

"Did any of you guys hear the howl last night after the one in the park?"

"Not me," Simba said.

"Not a thing," Remi said.

Roxie shook her head. "I didn't hear anything more."

"I forgot to listen," Meatloaf said.

Ooooooooooooooooooooooooooooooooo.

I told the pack what we'd found that morning. "I got news. Gizmo and I went over to Harley's place, we can confirm his disappearance."

"Harley? " Ranger asked. "I knew a dog named Harley. He was a big star in the movies. Hollywood, you know. In LA."

We ignored him.

I went on. "So then we went by to see Spike. He was his usual cranky self, but he told us he heard the twilight howl and saw Harley walk by his house. He said it sounds like Harley to him, too."

"When did Spike see him?"

"Last week, I think."

Roxie jumped up and down at the news. "Is he sure?"

"He said it was Harley."

Remi the spoil-sport didn't seem impressed. "Spike is old, thirteen or fourteen. His eyesight is failing, therefore he's not a reliable witness. It's more likely he saw a black coyote."

I didn't think coyotes came in black. And they certainly were skinnier than a Rottweiler.

Simba shuddered at the mention of our desert-dwelling brothers. "Coyotes scare me."

Ooooooooooooooooooooooooooooooooo.

"What is that creepy howl?" Ranger asked us again.

Finally we explained how we thought it was Harley askin' us to help him.

"Well, why don't we help him?" Ranger said.

"We're tryin' too," I said.

"Let's organize a search party," Ranger said. "You guys follow me, we can leave right now. I bet I can find him."

Meatloaf scoffed. "What makes you think so?"

"I used to lead search parties. I used to find lost children, my nose is extra strong."

Roxie hopped in the air. "That's great! Let's go."

Gizmo broke up the party. "Back off, Brownie. We don't follow you, Taser is our alpha dog."

Ranger looked at me with disdain. "Lazer's your alpha?"

"Taser," I said.

The thing about being an alpha is, you either are or you aren't. It's not somethin' you decide to be one day, you're born that way. And this mutt wasn't an alpha, I could always feel the pull. Near as I could tell, Ranger was all bark and no bite.

"Look Ranger," I said. "If we go runnin' off now, our owners will yell at us and make us come back. We got to sneak out when the time is right."

"You have to sneak? Why? My owner trusts my judgment."

I doubted that. "That's fine, but we're not even sure where Harley is."

Ranger pointed his nose out toward the mountains. "The howl came from out near the tallest mountain. Close to that first peak."

Gizmo scoffed. "Not possible. Harley's been gone over a week. No dog could survive a week out in that desert. Besides, Spike said it was the other direction."

Ranger looked at us like we were too stupid to show up at dinnertime. "Is something wrong with your hearing? It came from the mountains."

"No way. That's an echo. Besides, there's coyotes out there that would eat dogs in a minute. Not to mention Javelina pigs."

Ranger puffed out his chest. "So what. I'm not scared of wild pigs or coyotes. Where I came from, we used to hunt coyotes for entertainment."

"Where'd you come from?"

"LA, I told you. In California."

Meatloaf's ears perked up. "I'm from California. From Fresno."

"Frisco? San Francisco is cool. I been there."

"No, not Frisco, Fresno," Meatloaf said. "We weren't anywhere near the ocean."

"Fresno? Yuch." Ranger said. "I'm from Los Angeles, that's where it's happening."

Meatloaf looked confused. "What's happening?"

"Whatever's not happening in Fresno." He sniggered. "And trust me, nothing's happening in Fresno."

Meatloaf turned to me. "I don't like the new dog."

Ranger didn't act like he cared what Meatloaf thought. "That's fine, goofy. Who needs you?"

Then Remi opened his furry trap and threw in with the weasel. "I like Ranger. I see nothing wrong with his eagerness to help." He looked at Ranger like he was the new alpha.

Ranger nodded. "Thanks, Remi. That's one friend. And Simba here likes me. Don't ya gorgeous?" He stepped closer to my main mount. Simba didn't resist his advance, she looked like she was enjoying all the attention.

That was enough for me, I got right in Ranger's muzzle. "Hey buttsniffer, back off. Simba's my girl. And yeah, I'm the alpha of this pack."

Ranger stood tall and looked down his muzzle at me. "That was last week, Blaser."

"My name's Taser. Why don't you go back to Los Angeles?"

He stepped forward. "Why don't you make me?"

Rrrrrrrrrrrrrrrrr. I was just about to bite him, when…

"Wait! Please!" It was Roxie. "We shouldn't be fighting, we should be searching for Harley. I don't care who leads us. Harley doesn't care either."

I cared a lot, and I said so. "I'd rather follow a Siamese cat."

Ranger sneered. "Fine. We don't need you, Faser."

I got nose to nose with him. "It's Taser, you pure-bred loser."

All of a sudden the humans broke up their conversation, it was dark and time to go. Robert called our name.

Taser, Meatloaf!

Then I heard someone call out for Ranger, probably his owner.

Ranger! Come on, boy.

I let him go, we'd have to settle this some other time. Ranger ran over to the humans and started down the street. It was then I saw who his human was.

Oh no. It was Shannon.

I sat down and stared. "Meatloaf. Look."

He turned and saw what I saw. Ranger was walkin' down the street with Shannon. Ranger was our new neighbor.

"We got a problem here, Meat."

Meatloaf saw it. "A big problem." He lifted his leg on a bush and peed to punctuate our predicament.

SEVEN *Meanwhile, not too far away…*

Harley drank the last little bit of the water in his water dish, trying to avoid the little black bugs floating around on top. Finally he licked the last bit of moisture and didn't worry about bugs. Then he checked his food bowl again, but it was as empty as the last time he looked. He wandered toward the fence as far as his tether would allow, checking the dirt yard for scraps or any garbage he could eat.

Harley could hear cars behind the rear fence, he thought he was near the shopping stores. It didn't matter, he couldn't see them and they couldn't see him. He might as well be far away from his home. Thinking that just made him sadder.

He sniffed the air, it was the same strong smell, it had dulled his nose to little smells. At least the humans were gone.

He thought about his twilight howl. One of these times his friends would hear him. Maybe one time they would come to help him escape. It was Harley's only hope, and he clung to it.

He strained and pulled until the thick collar dug into his neck, but it was no use. These bad humans had him tied up tight and he wasn't ever getting free.

He lay down and put his head on his huge black paws. He didn't feel much like the big tough Rottweiler everyone thought he was. He thought of little Roxie for a while, missing her. He hoped she would never see him tied up and helpless like this.

He exhaled loudly, thinking of his friends playing at the park, then he thought about how he came to be at his Scottsdale home. It all started years ago when his second owner, Tim-Bop, got him that stupid collar name tag.

Harley was barely more than a year-old when these two crazy dudes bought him and…

***

South Phoenix, Two-years previous

Tim-Bop walked in the house with a brown bag in one hand. He set it on the table and reached in for a wide, flat jewelry box. He opened the lid carefully to reveal a large gold name plate. He held it up for Squiggy to see.

Shaggy squinted at the item in front of his face. "What the hell you got there?"

"Dog's new name tag." Thick gold letters were cast in simple script and joined where they touched to form the name HARLEY. The huge name-plate was about six-inches wide and three inches tall.

"What the hell you wastin' money on that fo?"

"Harley needs bling, same as anybody."

"Sheet. That is messed up."

Tim-Bop worked for ten minutes fastening and re-fastening the shiny tag to a new studded black leather collar while his friend tipped back a beer bottle. When he was done he held it up in front of the young black dog sitting and watching intently.

"Whatchew think, Harley?"

Shaggy answered for the Rottweiler. "Waste a money, that's what I think. Besides, that dog don't deserve no bling, he's a pussy. I as' you to get me a Rott-weiler, an' you done bring me a Pussy-weiler."

"Hey. Don't be hurtin' my dog's feelin's."

"So now he's your dog. Who paid for that mutt?"

"I'll pay you for him next month, I tole you that."

Harley sat next to the worn fabric couch and watched the two men argue. The arguing didn't bother Harley, they did that a lot when they drank. He was interested in the shiny new collar, but more interested in getting his dinner bowl filled. If they got to arguing too much he knew they'd forget.

Tim-Bop bent over and removed the old nylon collar from around Harley's neck. Then he attached the new leather collar with name

54

attached and stepped back to admire it. He stared, then bent back over to adjust it.

Shaggy watched him work. "While you down there, check and see if that dog's got any stones. I do believe he been neutered."

"He got more stones than you got."

"He's a pussy. I tried to get him to bite that bitch a mine yesterday and he wouldn't do it."

"Harley don' bite just anyone. He's discretionary." Tim-Bop beamed at big black dog.

Harley sat tall and proud with his new gold name tag. It was big, heavy and felt very important.

Shaggy sounded irritated. "Whatchew mean, dis-cretionary?"

"He's picky. He don' just bite on command, he needs a good reason."

"That so?"

Shaggy pulled a Glock out of his belt and pointed it at Harley. "Well I don' shoot just anybody but I just might shoot this dog. I certainly gots good reason. He shamed me in front of my bitch."

Harley growled at the black gun pointed in his direction. He didn't know why, the growl just came out of his mouth. He'd heard their guns fire at night before. They flashed bright and hurt his ears. He didn't like them.

Shaggy kept pointing at Harley. "Now the damn dog growlin' at me."

"He don't like guns. Put that shit away. You're not shootin' my dog anyhow."

"That's my dog an' I shoot him when I want."

"I'm warnin' you Shaggy, put that shit away before I hafta shoot you myself." Tim-Bop fished his own pistol out of his sagging pants and pointed it at the floor, his feet spread and facing his roommate.

Shaggy waved his own weapon in the air. "You like that dog so much you can pay me for him right now."

"You know I ain't got the money."

"But you got money for that dumb bling."

"A hunnert bucks off Willy. He says it's solid gold."

"My ass. He gets 'em from China for twenty bucks."

"It's solid gold, I tell ya."

"Shoulda give me the hunnert."

"I'll pay you for the dog next month."

"If you ain't got the money now that makes Harley my dog. An' I kin shoot my own dog whenever the dis-cretionary moment come over me."

"Shaggy, if you shoot that…"

Shaggy sighted the gun on Harley but Tim-Bop raised his weapon and pulled his trigger first.

BOOM!

The noise was deafening in the small room. Harley ran to his corner bed and put his head down.

Shaggy slumped over from a bullet hit but fired back at Tim-Bop.

BOOM!

Both men fell to the floor, one didn't move.

Harley cowered in his corner, unsure of what to do but terrified of the gunfire. When he raised his head to look, he saw his friends lying down. He smelled blood and gunpowder, then he heard labored breathing.

He got to his feet and walked slowly over to where the two men lay. Tim-Bop was wheezing, saying something. Harley stood a little closer, whined, and then went to the front door and started barking.

"WOOF WOOF WOOF WOOF!" "WOOF WOOF WOOF WOOF!" "WOOF WOOF WOOF WOOF!"

He turned around and looked at his friend, then kept barking. He didn't stop until the neighbors came, and then the police.

***

Doctor William Reed broke scrub and walked out in the waiting room, mask up and gloves off. He looked around and saw Officer Williams standing by the coffee machine holding a cup and talking to a nurse. He called out.

"Hey Tommy."

The officer turned around and asked. "How's the banger?"

Doctor Bill sighed. "Nine millimeter, he'll live. He'll probably be back next month, though."

"Yeah, well, you can use the practice with these boys. Unlike me."

The doctor smiled. "What's this about a Rottweiler?"

"From the shooting scene. I hated to leave him, and I heard what you said last week, so…"

"Is the dog here?"

"Back of the squad car, come see."

Doctor Bill stuck a dollar bill in a vending machine, pushed two buttons and collected something below.

They walked out to the cold Phoenix night. The back of Maricopa County Hospital was lit up like the holiday season. Doctor Bill looked up at the sky and breathed the fresh air in deep.

"This is probably not the best time for you," the officer apologized. "But I hated to take him to the pound at Christmas." He pointed at his Ford cruiser parked in the row of ambulances. "Over there."

Doctor Bill squinted. A black Rottweiler sat tall in the backseat, panting and watching the two men check him over. A huge gold name plate hung down from the dog collar, sparkling in the glint of holiday lights strung on the hospital back door.

"Harley, huh," Doctor Bill eyeballed the dangling tag. "He friendly?"

"To a fault. I'm afraid he won't make much of a watch dog. But he was pretty good at calling for help."

"Now all I need is a wife."

Tommy laughed. "Just get one that likes big sloppy dogs."

They walked up to the car and cracked the door. Harley sniffed the offered hand, then panted in approval as the Doctor reached in his

57

pocket for the packet of vending-machine crackers. He peeled the wrapper off and fed them to the hungry dog one by one. Harley accepted them daintily, along with some loving strokes on his head. Then Doctor Bill looked up.

"Thanks, Tommy. I'll take him. Besides, with that name tag he looks like he'll fit right in my neighborhood."

"Where's that?

"Scottsdale."

EIGHT *Saturday Morning*

The next day was not a shiny shoe day because Robert woke up late. When he didn't come down on time we complained a lot, finally our whining got him up. It was a different morning than our usual one. After we ate first meal, Robert went to the garage to leave.

Catcrap.

It looked like we were gonna be alone a while. Then he called out to us.

Taser, Meatloaf! Let's go.

We raced out and stood by the Jeep while he opened the big garage door. Meatloaf danced around in a complete spin to show how happy he was. I thought maybe we were goin' for a hike in the mountains, but Robert didn't bring any water bottles or hiking stuff. It didn't matter, any time we spent with him was great.

We jumped in the back and the Jeep pulled out. Then Robert stopped a minute and said somethin' funny out the window to the new female, Shannon. They laughed, then talked for a while and laughed a little more. Meat and I looked at each other, thinkin' our plan was working nicely. We were gonna have them mated in no time.

"Why doesn't he just mount her?" Meatloaf asked. "Females hang around the house after they get mounted. Sometimes it's hard to get them to leave."

I wasn't sure about that, but I told him what I'd learned on The Batchelor TV show.

"Humans don't immediately mount, they have to stare at each other's nose for a while."

Then Robert drove off down the street. I watched the houses go by and saw Gizmo was right, a lot of homes looked empty and had signs in the front yards. They also had weeds growin' and dead bushes in the yard. One of them had this weird spray-paint writing on the side wall.

We drove by a male and female human walkin' a mystery dog on a leash. It wasn't any mutt we knew, much less what breed it was. So me and Meatloaf stuck our heads out the window and let 'em have it good.

"BowWowWoofWoofBowWowWoofWoof!"

After we'd showed him who owned the neighborhood, we panted and drooled. I felt great after that. Then Robert drove out and went on the big road for a while.

The first stop was at Mack and Donald's house. We moved along the driveway until this nice lady leaned out the window and gave Robert a paper bag with somethin' that smelled great, but Robert ate it all. We would have gladly settled for the bag, but he didn't even offer us that.

After Mack's place, we stopped at the Big Home Store. Robert said somethin' about workin' on the house, but that's what Meat and I do every day, so I guess he was talkin' about himself. We went to sleep in the back of the Jeep while he went inside the store.

He came back with all these plastic bags and cans of stuff and then we went home. Robert took his bags to the burnt laundry room and started doin' things to the walls that smelled interesting for a while, but we got bored watchin' real quick. We may be Labradors, but we're not easily amused for long. We went outside because there's always things to see out there.

Through our fence I could see a Quail family walking by in single file, there musta been eight little ones tryin' to keep up. Then a lizard scurried across the patio, so I took off after him, but he disappeared under a bush like they always do.

Someday I'm gonna catch one of those little snakes with legs.

I stared at the bush a while, then I wandered out to sniff the grass.

Grass is amazing stuff. You can eat it when your stomach hurts, you can sleep on it, and you can poop on it. No wonder it's everywhere, even at the desert houses where we live. Not every house has it, probably because not every house has a dog. Me and Meat were lucky.

We slept a little. Ok, maybe we slept a lot, then we went in the house to find Robert.

It was Meatloaf who noticed it first.

He was watching Robert work. "He seems in a good mood. He seems awful happy today."

I looked, Meatloaf was right. I hadn't seen him this happy in a long while. He even gave us an extra bone early in the day. Then he put on some old-guy music, music kinda slow and soft. I didn't recognize the singer voice.

"What is that, Meat? Somebody is singin' about the country that Judy came from, New York."

Meatloaf lifted one ear. "It's franxinatra. I knew it."

"What?"

"He's got a date tonight. He puts on franxinatra music before he goes out on a date. Keep an eye on him. He'll take a water shower next."

I watched Robert closely, I saw he was cleaning up the mess in the laundry room. Then he moved around the house and put stuff away, even the dirty dishes. That was unusual. Next thing we know he went upstairs and then we heard the water runnin'.

"See," Meatloaf said. "He's going on a date with Shannon."

"That was fast."

Meatloaf nodded. "They been talking a lot ever since she moved in. He probably asked her to go out on a date when we saw her in the Jeep this morning."

I got excited thinkin' about that, I wanted Robert to be happy.

That was the good news. The bad news was we weren't goin' to the park tonight. I mean, he takes us almost everyday, but tonight was a special date night. I figured I could live with that sacrifice.

So we took a nap while we waited.

When he finally came down he had on his shiny-shoe work clothes. He gave us second meal and then went out to the garage. We heard the big door grinding sound, then the Jeep started. Soon we were all alone in the quiet house.

"I hate when he goes out," Meatloaf said, sighin' like an abandoned dog.

I sat in the livin' room with my nose stuck through the open shutter, watchin' the street carefully. I was worried because somethin didn't look right. "Hey Meat. Robert didn't drive over to Shannon's house, he drove down the street. You sure he's got a date with her tonight?"

Meatloaf stretched out on the carpet. "He's probably meeting her at a restaurant. Let's hope he brings us a doggy bag."

I liked the sound of that. "There's two people on this date. Maybe there will be two doggy bags."

"He might have one, but not her."

"Why not?" I asked.

"Female humans don't eat much on the first few dates. They like to pretend they don't care about food."

"That's weird."

"Tell me about it." Meatloaf went on. "They don't eat much until the male moves in with them. Then suddenly there's a lot more food in the house."

"That's good, right?"

"Real good."

"That's another reason to get Robert mated." I got a look in Robert's refrigerator when he made dinner one night. It was mostly beer, peanut butter and some old lettuce that had melted to the glass shelf.

Ok.

Now all we had to do was to kill time until Robert came home.

"You wanna watch the Animal Channel?" I asked Meat.

He yawned. "Nah. You go ahead."

So I went in to flip channels and got lucky. I found the Dizzy Dalmatian movie with all the black and white spotted puppies and the weird villain, this creepy female. So I'm watchin' that until it gets to

62

the sad part where they're gonna hit the puppies on their head and skin 'em. I hate those sad parts. So I shut it off, hit the dog door and went out back. Then I raised my nose and sniffed the desert.

Sniff-snifff-sniff.

Hmmmm.

I coulda swore it was coyote. It was hard to tell because it was so faint, but I thought it might be Dominga.

When I first met her she was very angry at humans. She seemed to have a hard life and she resented how dogs had it so easy, beggin' off man. She was right, but I didn't have much choice.

Soon though, Dominga and us dogs became almost friends. If not friends, we were two different animals that respected each other.

I lay down on the patio and waited.

Then I heard Meatloaf bark in the house. I ran in and planted my butt on the floor like I'd been there all night waitin' for my master to come home. That's dog rule number nine. Always appear happy to see your human.

Hey. I didn't make these rules, they came with my black coat.

I was so happy, my tail was waggin' like crazy, sweepin' the floor clean behind me.

Then Robert came in the door with this female. I don't know who it was but it wasn't Shannon from across the street. This was bad. She walked right past us, even though we were waggin' our tails and lookin' extra cute. They went into the kitchen for a while, opening cabinet doors like they were getting beer drinks or something.

There was lots of fun goin' on in there, but none of it involved Labradors. I didn't like it. And I didn't like her.

"What happened to Shannon?" I asked my buddy.

"I don't know. But I think we're in trouble," Meatloaf said. "Did you see her shoes?"

"No."

"Go look."

We were layin' low in the hallway. I got up and peered around the corner and saw the two drinkers in the kitchen. I turned back to Meat.

"I saw her shoes. What about them?"

"She's wearing ho-heels. Remember what I told you, when they want to get mounted they wear those ho-heels."

This didn't make any sense to me, but I deferred to Meatloaf's experience. He had the female owner for a while, not me.

"You think Robert is gonna mount her?"

"Maybe."

"But just because he mounts her, doesn't mean he'll mate her, right?"

"Right," Meat said. "It goes like this. First, there's a lot of mounting, and then they mate and move in together, then next there's not much mounting anymore."

It sounded strange to me, but I'm a dog. It didn't matter, I just didn't want the mate to be this female, I wanted Shannon.

"This female doesn't even seem to care about dogs," I said. "She didn't say anything to us at all."

"I know."

I looked at her again. "She's got a big chest and the golden hair that male's get stupid over."

"Taser, this is terrible."

There was a lot of laughing and drinking going on in the next room without us, which upset me a lot because they didn't try to bribe us with treats first to stay away.

"She walked by like we were a cat or something." It was a sad situation. "We need to get involved. We need to do somethin' to break this up."

"What should we do?" Meatloaf asked.

"Let's go stare at 'em, that always works."

So we snuck in the living room and sat close to the wall. By now Robert and Miss Ho-heels were on the couch. I thought at first they were staring at each other's noses, then I saw he was biting her on the mouth. It looked painful to me, but she seemed to be enjoying it.

64

Pretty soon she's laying on her back and he's holdin' her down like the vet is gonna give her a shot.

I thought Robert was gonna mount her for a minute, but she still had her clothes on. Somehow I didn't think that would work. I looked at Meatloaf for a clue, but he was staring closely at them, so I did too.

Just then the female looks over and sees us lookin'. She says somethin' to Robert so he gets up and gets a couple doggie treats out of the box in the pantry. Then he walked to the back door and threw them out on the patio.

Taser, Meatloaf. Outside.

We went out and got our bones and took them out on the grass to eat them. We munched a while before we talked again, but we were both thinkin' about Robert.

I looked up. "He's crabby about something."

"He wants privacy. They don't like when you watch."

"What happens next?" I asked. "Don't they hafta take their clothes off?"

Meat chewed the last of his doggie treat, then said. "It gets ugly. You don't want to know. And you definitely don't want to see."

I looked up when I saw them get off the couch and walk to the stairs.

"They're going up to Robert's bedroom," Meatloaf said. "It's all over for us."

"What do you think we should do?" I asked.

Meatloaf didn't say anything, so I waited. Finally I asked him again.

"I'm thinking," he answered.

This *really was* serious. I'd never seen Meatloaf think before. Finally he said something.

"Ok, I got it. We have to make it unpleasant for her. We don't want her living here. We need Shannon to be his mate. So if Ho-Heels thinks Robert has two disgusting dogs, she'll leave and never come back."

"Excellent. But we need a plan," I said. "What should we do, poop in the house?"

"That's good, but not personal enough. Robert will just pick it up and spray some magic water stuff on it. We need to get under Ho-heels skin, like a tic."

"Yeah." I tried to think of somethin' to do to her.

Meatloaf looked inside the house. "Is her purse in there?"

I could see through the big glass door that her purse was in the kitchen. "It's on the counter. What're you thinking?"

"Females are in love with their purse. They care more about their purse than their own mate. If we can pull her purse down on the ground we can chew it."

"Or pee on it," I offered.

"Better yet. Let's go."

We crept around the side of the house and snuck in the dog door. Once we got in the hall, we could hear them upstairs thrashing around like they were havin' a nightmare. I looked up the stairs and shook my head.

"I hope Robert's alright."

In the kitchen, Meatloaf was standing on his hind legs and tryin' to reach her purse with his teeth. He jumped and snapped his jaws, but still couldn't reach it.

"Let me try," I said.

Meatloaf got down and mumbled somethin'.

I put my paws on the edge of the counter and looked. I saw some mail letters, some car keys, the Ho-purse, and a plate with a couple leftover diner rolls.

I leaned way in and tried to bite it. It was no use. The purse was all the way to the rear of the counter.

"I can't reach it. We'll come up with a different plan."

He mumbled again

When I got back down on all fours, I saw Meatloaf had something stuffed deep in his mouth.

"Meat. What are you doing?"

"Mmmmnnnmmm. "

"Is that a dinner roll?"

"Mmmmmmmn."

"Try to stay focused. What do we do now?"

He finished chewing and swallowed. "Maybe we should bite her."

"Effective, but too drastic. We can save that for later. What if we chew her shoes, those Ho-heels? That should make her mad."

Meatloaf shook his head. "Naw. Females are always looking for a reason to by a new pair of shoes. This needs to be personal."

We sat down and thought and listened to the noise upstairs. I thought about Meatloaf's last owner, and how she got rid of him after he ate her favorite panties. Then all of a sudden it came to me.

"Meat. We need to eat her underwear. That makes 'em really, really mad, doesn't it?"

Meat looked scared. "Yeah, but I dunno, that's serious dog felony."

I volunteered for the crime. "I'll do it. You have a prior offense. I won't get in as much trouble as you would."

"You sure? You'll have to go upstairs and get them. That's two dog-felony counts."

I was committed. I'd had some bad owners already and I didn't want to let another bad female disturb our happy home. "Robert doesn't know what he's doin'. He just wants to mount this female, he wouldn't even care if someone turns the garden hose on him."

"Maybe we should try that."

I shook my head. "He's not the problem, males will mount anyone. We need to stick to the plan and get rid of her."

"Right." He thought a minute. "What's the plan, again?"

"I go upstairs, creep in their room and steal her panties while they're distracted. Then I'll bring 'em down to the living room and chew 'em up."

"Right." Meatloaf took a deep breath. "Go get 'em, dawg."

I padded up the stairs quietly, then crept to Robert's bedroom and nosed open the door. At first I worried that the underwear might be on the dresser or somethin', but there were clothes all over the floor.

67

I got down on my belly and did my best war-dog crawl over to the clothes pile. There was a lot of strange noises coming from the bed, but I didn't want to look. I scanned the floor, unsure of what female panties looked like. I sniffed Roberts clothes, then hers, then finally I found them. They weren't much bigger than one of Robert's socks.

I bit her underwear with my teeth and crawled back out the door and hurried down the stairs.

Meat was waiting. "You got em!"

I nodded and took them in the middle of the living room. I lay down with them between my paws and started to chew. Meatloaf came over to watch.

"Hey Taser," he said. "I been thinking. I can't let you take the rap for this. I'll chew her panties for you."

I looked up. "Meat, that's awful nice of you, but I can't let you do that."

"No, really. You don't want to get in trouble for this."

"It's alright, buddy. I'm not worried."

"I think too much of you to let you be punished for this."

I looked down at the underwear, then back at Meatloaf. "You're a true friend, but this is my sacrifice."

"You sure? I can take over."

"No, thanks."

He watched me a little longer, then said. "Taser, you're not doing it right. Better let me do it."

"Seriously, I got this."

"I'm the panty eater in this house."

"Not tonight."

He kept watching me, finally he blurted out. "How about sharing?"

"No way."

"Taser, give me those panties."

"Get out of here, they're mine."

"Mine!"

Meatloaf lunged and bit them and pulled. I pulled back and we had an instant tug-of war. We were growlin' and yankin' and all of a sudden they ripped in two pieces.

I stood up, panting from the fight. "You ripped them."

"*You* ripped them!"

"Pantystealer."

"Selfishdog.

We walked in a circle and then settled down on opposite sides of the room to each chew what was left of our two halves.

It wasn't long before we heard the water runnin' upstairs and thought it was time to hide. We left the chewed underwear on the carpet and ran out the dog door all the way to the back fence. Pretty soon Robert comes outside and holds the underwear scraps in front of our nose and says,

Who did this? Taser? Meatloaf?

We hung are heads like we were sorry, but we were only sorry about getting caught. Since we both looked guilty, he couldn't pin the rap on just one of us. It's one cool thing about having two Labradors in the house. Robert just looked at us and went back in the house.

Next thing we heard was the front door slamming.

"Is she gone?" Meatloaf asked.

I looked into the house. "I think so, her purse is gone."

"We did it."

"You mean *I* did it."

"Only because you wouldn't share."

"I stole 'em."

"You weren't doing it right."

"Pantystealer."

"Selfishdog."

NINE   *Sunday Morning*

The next morning I heard the doorbell ring very early, even before the news papers lady drove by. Since no one was up but me, I let out a bark to warn Robert. Then I went over to the window and nosed open the shutter. It was hard to see, but I thought it was a female. I worried Miss Ho-heels comin' back to make trouble for us, but then I smelled it was our new neighbor.

"Who is it?" Meatloaf asked.

"It's Shannon. Somethin' must be wrong."

The doorbell rang again, so I let out a couple more barks.

"WOOF WOOF!"

Sometimes I scare myself.

Taser!

It must be someone Robert knows, because he was applyin' Rule #8. Don't bark at people you know. But I couldn't help it.

Robert came downstairs half-dressed, wearing his short pants.

He opened the door and let Shannon in. She seemed upset about somethin'. She was wearing baggy denim pants and hiking boots, so I knew she was definitely not in heat this morning. She was talkin' so fast it was hard to understand her words. I cocked my head and raised one ear.

Sorry…bother…last night…park…desert…help…

"What's she saying, Taser?"

"Quiet. I'm still listenin'."

She had some problem and she was comin' to Robert for help, that much I understood.

Ranger…out…away…lost…

"Hey Meat," I said. "Looks like Ranger ran away."

70

"Good riddance. Maybe he went back to California because we're so boring over here."

They were still talkin', so I kept listenin'. She really talked a lot, but I got a good understanding of what happened, so I told Meatloaf.

"Meat, get this. Last night after dinner, Ranger got out of the backyard. Shannon heard the gate slam so she went after him. He ran down to the park and snuck through the drain pipe into the desert. Then the idiot ran off toward the big mountain. She waited, but he never came back."

"Good."

"She thought he might come home late at night, so she left the gate open in case he returned, but he's vanished."

"Wow."

At first I was glad to get rid of him, then I realized something. "That makes two."

"Two what?" Meatloaf asked.

"There's two dogs missing now in the neighborhood. What's goin' on, Meat?"

"I dunno. Is something going on?"

"It's not safe for dogs around our neighborhood anymore. First Harley and then Ranger."

"Come on. They just ran away, that doesn't count as missing. Besides, Ranger was a jerk."

My buddy was right, Ranger was a jerk. But he was still a dog. I felt bad for him. "You know what Meat, I think he went lookin' for Harley."

"He doesn't even know Harley."

"Yeah, but he's such a know-it-all, maybe he wanted to show us up by findin' Harley."

"I hope the coyotes ate him."

"That's cold, buddy. You gotta have more compassion for our kind."

I knew Ranger might have got eaten because two coyotes almost ate me one time. I could see them wanting to eat Meatloaf because he looked like a porkchop, but I was all muscle. Maybe they couldn't tell by looking—or maybe they'd eat anything. Either way, I didn't want to find out.

Robert said good bye to Shannon and went back upstairs. We whined because he forgot to feed us, but he came back in a minute dressed like Shannon was, heavy pants and boots. I figured we were goin' for a hike. He fed us and then he ate some cooked bread while we waited by the front door.

Next Robert knelt down on one knee and talked to me all serious, like it was a matter of life and death.

Taser. Find Ranger.

He held Ranger's leash by my nose so I could sniff the scent. Not that I didn't have the idiot's smell in my brain already.

Find Ranger.

Then he put both of us on long leashes and we went out the door toward the park. I was really pullin' hard on my leash because I was happy to have a job doin' stuff to help Robert. I was so proud I didn't care we were lookin' for a dog I didn't like.

We hustled down to the park and sniffed the grass. It was easy to single out Ranger's scent because he was the new dog. His smell took us right to the big drain pipe. I stuck my nose inside, then turned and looked at Robert. He unhooked our leashes and we started through, but I stopped and sniffed at one spot inside the pipe that was strong with coyote scent. It was their pee. The pipe was wet from the morning's sprinklers and all the smells seemed intense in there.

When we came out, we saw Robert throw something over the wire fence, then jump over and pick it up. It was a baseball bat, I guess in case of coyote trouble. He had a water bottle on his belt, too. He looked at me and pointed out in the desert.

Find Ranger.

72

It was on me, now. I had the best nose in our pack and it was time for me to use it.

I got Ranger's scent off the bushes along the trail that headed toward the big McDowell Mountain peak. The ground was rocky and gravelly, but our pads were pretty tough from running in the street and digging in the yard. People had hiked up here before, so we knew where to step. The rocks were small on the trail itself, kinda like our neighborhood desert lawns.

The thing you gotta watch out for in the desert is cactus, especially those Cholla jumpin' cactus. You only need to smell them one time and wham, a needle right in the nose. That's the last time you get near one of those.

Needles in your paw pads are even worse, that's why Robert brings pliers.

Then the bushes thinned out and the trail got thin, so I put my nose down closer to the ground and kept sniffin' and moving. Robert and Meatloaf followed close behind me. I smelled a bunch of quail and the desert mice and the rabbits, but I ignored them all. But when I picked up a new scent of coyote, I stopped in my tracks and looked at my master.

Robert knelt down next to me and put his hand on my back, stroking my coat. I was trembling under his gentle touch, all my senses on alert.

What is it Taser?

Heennnnngggg. Heennnnngggg.

Find Ranger, boy.

OK, but I warned you.

I stuck my nose back on the ground and we kept going in spite of coyote smell. I didn't know how old it was, maybe yesterday's scent, maybe from earlier in the day. It's hard to mistake coyote smell. It's very distinctive, kinda like wet dog and old meat poop.

The higher up the trail we went, the sharper the rocks underfoot got, and the harder it was to follow the smell of Ranger. But the worst part was, Meatloaf was startin' to limp bad. I hoped he'd be able to get back, he was too heavy for Robert to carry very far.

We reached a spot next to a Palo Verde tree where a bunch of little leaves fell on the ground. They felt good on my pads after the walk. I picked up strong scent all around that spot, so I figured Ranger spent some time under the tree. I walked around in a circle underneath and whined to show Robert it was important. He looked closely on the ground and then looked up the trail. It was gettin' steep and Meatloaf was limpin' so much I didn't think we should go any higher.

Robert pulled his water bottle off his belt, bent down and poured some in his hand for us to drink. First Meatloaf drank and then me. We were pantin' from the exercise, but not too much because it wasn't hot up there at all.

We had a nice breeze in our face, but it kept switchin' scents on me, which wouldn't let me relax and enjoy the moment. I tried to identify a different smell, somethin' didn't seem right. Smells are important, but my ancient dog sense helps warn me too.

Robert drank some out of the water bottle himself and put it away. We looked down on the Scottsdale city houses for a while, then finally we stood up and started back home. I was glad to leave the area because things seemed out of whack, I wasn't sure why.

Let's go home, guys.

Meatloaf led the way, then Robert, then I followed a little behind. We hadn't gone very far when my senses flooded alert. Maybe it was my danger sense, maybe it was something else, but I stopped and looked one side, then the other, and then I turned around.

The threat was behind us.

A skinny gray coyote stood at the top of the trail, standin' at the same spot we just left. It was staring at me with its cold eyes like it wanted somethin', probably a meal judging how thin it was. But skinny was normal for most coyotes, so I didn't think that was it. Maybe it wanted water. I wasn't afraid because it didn't seem menacing, just forceful.

74

I thought about barkin' but I didn't want to antagonize it, it probably thought we were invading its territory. Which was exactly what were were doin'. So I hustled to catch up to Robert and Meat down the trail to get out of there.

Further down, I turned around one last time to see the coyote still standin' up there, still watching me closely. It was creepy. I didn't say anything to Meatloaf though, I kept it to myself.

There was somethin' about it that really bothered me. I just couldn't put my paw on it yet.

***

When we got home, Robert put us in the house and went over to talk to Shannon alone. I thought that was a shame, I would have liked to hear that conversation.

We drank a bunch of water and sprawled on the tile, pantin' and droolin'. Robert stayed over there a while, I figured Shannon was real upset so they were talkin' about it. I know how upset I was when I lost a master, humans must feel the same about losing us dogs. Probably worse.

I told Meatloaf what I was thinkin'. "That Ranger is a real catbrain. What's he doing goin' out in the desert like that?"

Meat agreed. "He thinks he's some California superdog. He says used to hunt coyotes for entertainment."

"I don't believe half of what he says."

"I don't believe that much."

I scoffed. "You think he's really from LA?"

"So what if he is? LA is nothing special." Meatloaf thought a minute. "Neither is Fresno, I guess."

"I like where we live now."

Then I asked the question we both were both thinkin'. "You think the coyotes got him?"

"We didn't see any sign of that. I didn't smell any blood."

75

"Yeah, but Meat, come on."

"Maybe he fought 'em off."

I thought. "One maybe, not two or three. Not a pack. If he's dead it will be horrible. If he's just in trouble we should help him."

"Why? Why do you care?" Meatloaf asked. "He's after Simba. He challenged you in front of your pack. He lies. He's nothing but trouble."

"All true."

"Then why?" he said, yawning from his spot on the floor.

"Shannon won't like our neighborhood if her dog dies. She won't want to mate with Robert and live here."

"Fine. I ain't livin' with that dog, anyway."

I was with my buddy on that part, but the fact was I cared more about somethin' else.

Ranger was a dog, he was one of us.

***

Later that night, after second meal, I wondered outside. It was quiet, I couldn't hear nothin' but the murmur of neighbor television sets and distant wind chimes. I stared at the faint outline of the McDowell Mountain peak and thought about that lone coyote.

It felt like it was talkin' to me on a level we both shared, not dog to coyote, but creature to creature. Like we were brother animals in the struggle of life. I didn't wish coyotes any harm, they wanted to live, just like I do. Just like Ranger does. Or did.

I walked in a circle and lay down on the patio. It was cooler and it smelled a bit like rain. I stared out in the darkness, waiting like my senses told me.

Many minutes passed, I didn't move.

Then it came right at me.

Two glowing yellow eyes danced as they moved between the creosote bushes far out in the desert. The creature moved quickly, like it knew just where it was goin' and didn't have time to waste. When the coyote got within a ball's throw, it stopped and looked at me. It waited a moment, then slowly walked closer until I could see its face.

It was Dominga.

She was about my height, skinny but not as skinny as the last time I saw her. Her ears stood straight up, forming two tips of the triangle completed by her pointed snout. Her eyes offered neither warmth nor trust. But there she was at my fence, trusting me again.

Or did I need to trust her?

"Dominga." I asked. "Was that you on the mountain?"

She nodded, then answered in her strange coyote voice. "You came to search for your brother?"

"Ranger. Yes, we did. Is he alive?"

"He lives. But he is hurt. He needs help."

"Where! Where is he?"

She looked left and right, appearing nervous to possible danger from humans. "He is on the mountain. He fell into a deep gully. He is trapped there and needs your help."

I thought of what a tempting treat a helpless Labrador would be to hungry predators. I voiced my fears. "The other coyotes, they haven't hurt him?"

"No. Ikal and Seti watch over him. They will protect him from others until you come."

"Who are they? Who are Ikal and Seti?"

"They are my sons."

"Sons. You mean…"

"Last year. The time of no rain, when there was no food for us. You shared your food and saved my small ones from death. When the rains came back, they grew strong. Now they protect your kind in return."

"I see."

I had helped Dominga when no one else would, but I had gotten in trouble with my pack for feeding coyotes. Now it had come back to help us dogs.

77

"Your humans try to kill us. Other animals chase us, hurt us. Only you would help coyotes." She sat very straight. "So. You will come for him on the mountain? Come past the place you saw me watching."

"Yes, but…" I didn't know what I could do to get him out. "But how can I save him? Can you help?"

"No. He snarls at us. He does not trust coyotes to be close. It must be you and your fat friend."

"Meatloaf? No, his leg is weak and sore."

"Then you must come alone," she said.

"Yes." I thought quickly. "Next day in the day light."

"I will tell my sons."

She started to leave.

I called after her. "Dominga, wait. I need to ask you, have you heard the evening dog howls?"

She stared at me. "Three howls as the light dies?"

"Yes. Where do they come from?"

"The howls come from your dens."

"Do you know where? Do you know which house?"

"Ikal and Seti know this. My sons walk your wide trails at night hunting your fat rabbits."

"I'll ask them when I come for Ranger."

She walked a few steps, then turned around for a last appeal. "Taser. You must come soon. Your friend grows weak."

Then she was gone.

TEN *Monday Morning*

I woke up early to layout my plan to save Ranger. It was no problem getting' out of the house and our sideyard gate, the problem was figuring the best time to do it. I thought I better leave right after Robert did and head directly up the mountain. I had no idea how I was gonna help Ranger when I got there, I had to go see what I could do.

I drank plenty of water because I wasn't sure how long I would be gone. I hoped it wouldn't be overnight. I knew everyone would worry if I didn't come home. Besides, it wasn't safe out there in the dark time. When it got dark the bad stuff came out to hunt.

At first meal I only ate half of my food, then I let Meatloaf eat the rest. He looked at me funny, so I told him I didn't feel well. I don't like runnin' right after I eat. Or fighting.

I would fight a coyote, but a pack of Javelina pigs sent me runnin'. They'd charge and kill me as soon as they saw me. But I didn't worry about them too much, I always knew when they were around. Of all the desert animals, they smell the absolute worst. Stink isn't bad enough to describe it. Rotten, or dead would be better.

When I saw Meatloaf get sleepy, I snuck out the dog door and went to the gate. I backed up a bit, then ran and flipped at it with my nose. I missed the first time, but the second time it flipped up and I was out. I didn't wait to see if Meatloaf heard me, I took off joggin' toward the park. It was only four or five houses away.

It turned out I wasn't the only one there.

The city workers were all over the park, cuttin' trees and cleanin' leaves, but I ignored them and headed straight for the drain pipe like I knew what I was doin'. I didn't hafta worry, the worker guys in floppy hats ignored me and I scooted right through. Once on the desert trail I didn't need to follow my nose, I knew exactly where to go.

79

My foot pads were still tender from our first trip up the trail, so I limped some and it slowed me down. The rocks grew sharper as the elevation increased, but I put the pain out of my brain. I kept movin', tryin' only to think of Ranger down in a ditch, probably hurt worse than me.

After a while I stopped and panted, then turned around to see where I'd been. It seemed I was pretty high up. I was a little nervous without Robert to look out for me, but it had to be done. When I felt stronger I pushed on. The sun shown brightly but the air was cool.

Suddenly this horrible desert thing appeared on the edge of the trail. It looked like a giant version of the little lizards that run around our patio, except there was no way I was gonna chase after this thing. Or catch it. It had a huge mouth and a fat striped body and a stubby tail, maybe half as long as me. I'd never seen anything like it, I didn't want to ever see one again. My senses told me to be careful, very careful.

Whatever it was probably didn't think Labradors were cute, I was sure. I sat down and thought what to do.

At that moment I would have traded my sense of smell for better paws. Humans could use their paws to hit this thing with a stick or throw a rock at it. All I could do was bite it, but I was sure this ugly creature would bite me back.

Then I realized something.

If I ran fast enough, maybe I could get by the thing before it bit me.

I backed up some then started runnin'. When I got close, it suddenly spun around and ran under a rock. I zipped right by, proud of scaring somethin' so awful ugly. I didn't slow down until I was far away. When I looked around, it was nowhere in sight.

So I kept goin'.

It took a while, but I finally reached the spot where Robert and Meatloaf and I stopped last time. I sat under the same tree and rested awhile. I looked down the mountain, it seemed I was very high up.

But Dominga said I had to go higher. I looked up the trail for her. I hoped she might show up to lead me to the right spot, but there was no coyote in sight.

I walked further up. It was slow goin' now, but I finally reached a crest where I could see down three sides of the mountain. Trees were blooming and new flowering plants were everywhere. I used my eyes and my nose to search around them. My eyes helped me see a coyote nearly hidden as it blended perfectly in the desert.

He was off the trail, just sittin' and watchin'. Waiting for me, maybe. I didn't move, I kept lookin' for Ranger but he was nowhere to be seen. I thought he had to be close, so I barked.

"WOOF."

I waited, then barked again.

"WOOF."

The coyote hadn't moved. I cocked my head and listened good.

woof woof

It was faint, but I thought it was Ranger. I moved to the trail edge and looked down.

Then I saw him.

Ranger had fallen off the trail. The side of the hill was loose stones and gravel, so he'd slid all the way to the bottom. He was layin' in a little gully at the bottom of the hill. It looked like he was stuck, wedged against a tree or somethin'.

I tried to walk down to where he was, but I slid on the loose rock myself. He musta heard me before he saw me, 'cause he raised his head and barked weakly.

"Help!" Over here!"

I finally got down next to him and looked him over. I didn't see any blood or funny bent legs.

"Ranger, are you hurt?"

He was covered in desert dust and burrs. He looked at me through exhausted eyes. "Razor? Is that you?"

"It's Taser, you idiot."

81

"How'd you find me?"

"Don't ask," I said. " You got anything broken?"

He whimpered like a lost puppy. "I don't think so. It's my collar, it's caught on something."

I looked at his collar to find the problem. He'd slid into a low-hanging Palo Verde tree whose branches touched the ground. One of the thick branches slid under his collar, trapping him in place. He couldn't turn his head or slide free of it.

It was a mess, but I didn't want to worry him yet.

"Can you move your legs?"

He wiggled his body and thumped his tail on the ground. "Everything works, I think. I just can't move my head or get up."

"Lemme work on that," I told him.

"You gotta hurry, there's coyotes all over the place. They keep coming back to see if I'm dead yet."

"No Ranger. These coyotes are watchin' out for you. They're protectin' you."

"Yeah, they're protecting their next meal."

I wasn't gonna waste energy arguing with him. It looked like the only solution was to get his collar off, and that was gonna be a problem. I knew the thick nylon collar-stuff couldn't be chewed in half. I couldn't get my mouth around it anyway. I racked my brain. I wished Robert or another human was here, they always know the right thing to do. But wishing wasn't gonna help Ranger.

He kept complaining. "There's snakes, too. One of them slid right by my nose with all that scaly skin and a big rattle on its butt. I think I pissed myself."

"That's the least of your problems."

"Easy for you to say."

I ignore it and looked close at his collar. "We gotta get you off this branch. Can you push yourself uphill? I'll hold onto the branch until you slip off."

"I'll try."

"Wait." I got downhill from his body, planted my feet and bit on the branch. "Ok, push up."

I held the branch while he pushed with his legs, but the loose rock just slid out under his feet. He was heavy, probably ninety pounds, and he didn't move uphill easily.

I stopped. "Well, that didn't work." I thought. "Let me try to pull the branch out from under your collar. Brace yourself."

Next, I grabbed the branch with my teeth and yanked like I was playin' tug-a-war. It wouldn't move much, it was too thick. Ranger just slid down on the branch tighter.

I stopped and panted, starting to worry. I sensed he was weakening. "Maybe I should go back and get a human."

"Who?" he asked. "Shannon is at work."

"Robert will be home near dark-time." But then we'd have to come up in the dark, and I knew humans couldn't see then.

"We might not get back until next-day."

"I...I really need some water." Ranger said. "I don't know if I can go another day. Is there anything you can do?"

"Let me think." I looked up the hillside. The coyote was still there on the ridge, sitting on his haunches, watching us try to get free. He couldn't help us, but I was glad he was there. Somehow I didn't feel so helpless, but I knew I really was.

I looked at Ranger. "Why'd you come up here?"

"I wanted to find Harley," he said. "I thought you guys would accept me if I rescued your friend."

"You didn't have to do that. You'd have less problems fitting in if you weren't such a braggart."

He sighed. "I'm a jerk, right? You can say it."

"Yeah, you acted like a jerk. What's with all those lies? You probably never hunted coyotes, did you?"

"Nope. Coyotes scare me."

"Are you really from Los Angeles?"

"I'm from Barstow."

"Lemme give you a tip, Ranger. No one cares where you're from."

"Really? I do."

"Are you are a registered pure-bred?"

"Not really."

"A rescue Lab?"

"Technically, I never spent any time in the pound. But I was alone in the house a couple times."

I took a deep breath. "Ok. Now is not the time to worry about that. We gotta see what we can do to get you out of here."

"How's it look?"

"Not good."

He whimpered. "I knew it." Heennngg Heennngg.

"Ranger, don't give up."

"I'm not worth it. Just leave me for coyote chow. Save yourself, Quasar." He started cryin' like a newborn pup who couldn't find a nipple.

"Shut up." I looked at his collar again. If I couldn't chew his collar off, maybe I could chew the branch in two. It looked big, but Labradors are great chewers. Ask any Lab owner. But don't ask my Robert, that's a sore subject.

I stood up to go around him.

Ranger tried to move his head to see what was happening. "Wayser, where you going? You're not actually gonna leave me, are you?"

"No, I'm gonna chew on this branch."

"This is not the right time to amuse yourself."

"I'm gonna chew this branch in half. I gonna try, anyway."

It couldn't be any harder to do than the wood legs on our living room coffee table. But that's different *No-No, Bad Dog* story.

I picked a spot near where the tree branch went under the collar and started chewin'. The wood was new growth, still fresh from recent rains. I thought it might work. I chewed and swallowed, chewed and swallowed. The branch got a little smaller, but the wood chips tasted terrible.

Ranger lay there letting me work to get him free. He looked so pathetic I felt sorry for the dumb mutt. I started to change my opinion of him. I knew how much trouble I had fitting in when I was new-dog at the pound. Maybe Ranger wasn't such a jerk after all.

"I can't thank you enough for this," he said weakly. "I'll never forget all you've done for me."

I spit out a thorn. "Save it." I kept chewin'.

"No, really," he said. "Simba told me you were a hero. I heard how you saved your human from the house fire one night. I guess I was jealous. I wanted every dog to look up to me, like they look up to you."

I tried to ignore him, but he wouldn't shut up.

"I know I shouldn't tell lies, but it's not my fault." Ranger whimpered. "I've never told anyone this, but I came from a broken home. I never knew my father, I was raised by a single mother. You see, I was one of six or seven puppies. I barely got to know my brothers and sisters before they abandoned me one by one. Then finally, MY MOTHER GAVE ME AWAY!"

Ranger really started whimperin' at that.

I stopped to set him straight. "Hey Ranger, that's the way it works. The breeder's bitch has the litter..."

"Please." He acted all insulted. "Don't interrupt me, I'm pouring my heart out here."

I went back to chewin' and Ranger went back to talkin.

"So I went from my mother's loving paws to some strange male and female humans in another house, and the first they did was LOCK ME IN A METAL CAGE with only water to drink! When I finally got out of there and peed on the carpet, THEY SHOVED MY NOSE IN IT AND CALLED ME A BAD DOG! And then..."

The day wore on, the branch got smaller, and his sad life story got longer.

85

When he was finally done talkin', the branch felt thin enough where I chewed it. I crunched down hard and it broke in two. The front part fell away and his collar popped off the branch.

Ranger raised his head and struggled to his feet. "You did it! You saved me!" He shook his coat like a dog after a bath. "Wow! I've really been wanting to do that."

I was a little woozy from all the chewin'. My jaws hurt and my gums were bleeding, but it was done. Now we just had to get up the hill and go home.

I turned around and looked, the coyote was still there. It had to be one of Dominga's sons, I wasn't sure which one.

I pointed my nose up the hill. "Let's try to get up on the trail. Are you strong enough?"

Ranger sighed. "I don't know."

"Well, try hard."

We started up, slipping on the loose rock as we stepped. We'd make some good progress only to slide back down. We were halfway up when Ranger slid backwards into me and down we went. We ended up where we started, at the bottom of the ravine. We needed a new plan if we were gonna get out of there.

I pointed with my nose. "Let's follow the ravine down, maybe we can get to some solid ground."

Ranger balked. "Forget it. That's where the rattlesnake went."

"It's the only way out of here." I was tired of his complainin'. "You wanna go home or what?"

"I'm tired. I need water. I want my master. Heennngg Heennngg—"

I cut him off. "You candy-butt, shut your muzzle and get behind me."

Chocolate Labs.

I went first, steppin' over bigger rocks and hoppin' over the deep crevices. Soon it was mostly sandy bottom from the rain off the mountain. I turned to check, Ranger was right behind me.

86

Then we saw our way up. We found a section made of harder rock that let us climb to the trail. I sent Ranger up, then followed a ways behind. When we got to the top we sat and rested.

"You alright?" I asked him.

He panted. "Yeah. I could use some water, though."

"Soon. But right now I need to run up the trail a bit."

"What for?"

"I gotta see this coyote."

"What coyote?"

"The one who's been watching us the whole time." I pointed up the trail with my muzzle. "Look at the top of the ridge. See him?"

He looked and looked until he spotted the grey shadow nearly hidden among the granite boulders. "Well, I'll be a Doberman's uncle. How come he didn't eat us?"

"He's a friend, and right now I need to talk to him about something."

Ranger looked at me like I was crazy. "Coyotes can talk? Get out of here, you're pulling my leg."

"Just sit here and wait for me, ok Bandit?"

"Bandit?"

"Just stay here."

Ranger lay down in the shade.

I went further up the trail, past where Ranger had slid off, then moved even further up until I got close to the waiting coyote. I walked up to him cautiously because I didn't want to scare him. But he didn't act afraid of me in the least. He looked in good shape for the rough life he'd led, but he was still young.

This coyote had long spindly legs, and he was probably as tall as me. He was very thin through his chest and body, like he'd been squeezed between two cars. He was mostly grey with a sprinkle of brown hairs, a couple scars. His coat did look better then his mother's, though.

I spoke first. "Are you one of Dominga's sons?"

"I am Ikal."

His scent was strong, like his mother. He sounded like her, too. He had that weird coyote accent, probably because his muzzle was so narrow, but I understood his words.

I said, "She said you know our neighborhood."

"We walk your wide trails to hunt your rabbits. They are easy hunting, fat and lazy like your kind."

"I'm not lazy." I didn't argue the fat part. Compared to Ikal, I was tubby. Maybe I did eat too much. My stomach hurt right then, that much I knew.

"Our mother said you are a brave fighter. She said you killed Tajo, one of our best hunters."

I nodded, it was true. "Tajo wanted to eat me. I wanted to live."

"All animals want to live, but some will die because they are weak."

I couldn't argue with that, so I said nothing.

Then Ikal said, "Our mother said you gave us food to help us live."

"Yes," I said. "When you were pups. Where is your brother?"

"Seti hunts. We always hunt." He angled his huge pointed ears toward me. "What do you need from us?"

"I want to find Harley, the dog who lives next to my house. He howls for help near dark-time."

He looked right and left, then spoke. "I have heard his cry. We have heard his dog talk."

"Do you know where it comes from? Do you know which house?"

"It is not far from your den. It comes from the place of bad smells."

This was new information to me. "Bad smells?"

"Seti and I will come to your den. We will show you the way."

"When?"

"Soon. When the moon is dark." He turned to leave. "I must go."

I wanted to let him know how much I appreciated what they'd done for us. I started to tell him. "I'm thankful you and your brother watch—"

But he was gone.

It was awful late, I knew we had to get back, so I jumped up and trotted over to where to where I'd left Ranger. I didn't see him at that spot, so I looked off the road, then I looked far down the trail.

There was no sign of him anywhere. I sat down, totally confused. The Chocolate Labrador had vanished.

ELEVEN *Monday Afternoon, earlier*

Yaaawwwn.

Meatloaf stretched, then rolled on his back. He thought about second meal, and then his buddy. Taser should be back by now, he thought, but he hadn't heard him come in the house. On the other hand, Meatloaf didn't hear anything when he slept.

Yaaawwwn.

Taser, what a character. Always investigating something in the neighborhood. Probably he and Gizmo were up to no-good. That Jack Russell was another character. Those two probably walked to the far end of the subdivision searching for that big dumb Rottweiler. Why they wanted him back was a mystery, all Harley did was bark.

On the other hand, Harley did help the pack catch the murder-human. He was a good dog to have on your side. And he was their neighbor.

Maybe all dogs were good.

Taser seemed to think so.

Yaaawwwn.

He thought maybe Taser was in the other room watching the Animal Channel.

Meatloaf felt lonely, so he got up to look for Taser. He walked through all the rooms in the house and then went outside. Nobody was there either.

Meatloaf started to worry so much his stomach hurt, so he ate some grass.

He worried because Taser should have been home by now, it was almost time for Robert to come in the door. Taser was gonna miss his dinner if he wasn't careful.

Meatloaf walked to the sideyard gate and pushed on it with his nose. It swung open, unlatched. He stuck his head out and looked up and down the street. There was no sign of Taser or Gizmo. Meatloaf backed into the yard and sat down, unsure of what to do next. Robert wasn't gonna like this one bit.

It seemed like a good time to eat some of his seed pod stash.

***

When he heard the big garage door open, Meatloaf was sitting in the hallway, waiting. Robert came in carrying his briefcase.

Hi buddy.

Robert looked around.

Where's Taser?

He put his briefcase down, went in the kitchen, and then the living room. Meatloaf followed right behind, waiting for the catpoop to hit the fan.

Taser!

Then Robert went outside.

Taser!

He walked all around the outside of the house. He looked at the unlatched side gate and then back at Meatloaf sitting and watching.

Meatloaf looked away.

I had nothing to do with it. Honest.

Robert shook his head. He looked around for a rock, and then put it at the base of the gate to keep it ajar.

That dog, I swear.

Robert went back inside, opened the refrigerator and removed a bottle. He popped the top and took a long drink. The distinct smell hit Meatloaf's nose. Beer. Meatloaf thought beer must be the solution to almost everything. It always seemed to appear in a crisis.

Robert scooped a big cup of Eukanuba weight-control dog food and put it in a dog dish. Then he dropped a large white pill in on top of the food. Meatloaf eyed him suspiciously.

Glucosamine, Robert said. He held the bottle up for Meatloaf to see. *For your leg.*

Robert sprinkled the food with water and put it down on the floor, then stepped out of the way while Meatloaf inhaled the bowl contents.

Next Robert put a sauce pan on the kitchen stove. He went in the pantry and returned with a box and a jar from the shelf. Meatloaf watched hopefully, but when Robert popped the lid on the jar and Meatloaf got a whiff, he plopped down on the floor in disgust.

Oh great. Spaghetti. On top of everything else, no leftovers tonight.

Robert heated the sauce and boiled some water, then set one plate on the table. Meatloaf thought Robert seemed lonely, so he lay very close. Every now and then Robert look outside to see if Taser was back. Finally Robert ate his dinner, then he got a leash out of the drawer and motioned to Meatloaf.

Let's look at the park.

Meatloaf ran out the door and down the street, looking at each house on either side of him as he ran. There was no sign of his wandering friend. He figured Robert wanted to talk to the other dog owners at the park about it. Maybe they knew something the dogs didn't. That left Meatloaf to talk to the animals.

When they got to there, Gizmo was chasing a ball, so Meatloaf ran over to him.

"Hey Gizmo! You seen Taser today?

"Eh-eh." Gizmo spit the tennis ball out of his mouth. "Why, isn't he with you?"

"He left this morning. I thought he was out searching for Harley with you. But he never came home." Meatloaf looked over at the cluster of humans talking in their group. "Robert's upset."

"Maybe Simba's seen him." Gizmo looked over to where the Golden Retriever stood sniffing the grass. "Let's ask her."

They ran over to talk to Simba. She pulled her nose off the ground and smiled when she saw them. "Hi there."

"Did Taser come see you today?" Meatloaf asked. "He's not at the house, hasn't been there all day."

Simba lost her smile. "Oh no. What's he up to now?"

Meatloaf sighed. "I think he's looking for Harley. But I guess he could be looking for Ranger."

Gizmo cocked his head in question. "Why would he be looking for Ranger?"

"Oh, I forgot to tell you. Ranger ran away yesterday."

Simba and Gizmo spoke at the same time. "What?"

"Ranger took off."

"What's that?" It was Winston, waddling up to the group of dogs. "That idiot Ranger ran away? Stupid blighter. Does he think he's going to find a nicer place to live than right here?"

"I don't know if that's true anymore." Simba looked upset. "Now there's three dogs missing in the neighborhood. Harley, Taser and Ranger."

"I told you," said Winston. "The neighborhood's turned dodgy. There's something strange going on. Dogs disappearing, home burglaries, mysterious house fires. A disturbing trend for sure."

"You can blame the recently-arrived, lower-income element." Remi said, as he joined their discussion. "Vandals. Criminals. Low-lifes living among us now, possibly right next door. Absolutely terrifying."

Meatloaf tried to calm everyone down. "It's not that mysterious. Ranger's owner Shannon came over yesterday and said he ran out in the desert. He ran out toward the tall mountain peak. So Robert, me and Taser went up the McDowell Mountain trail yesterday to look. We found his scent but didn't find him."

"The coyotes must have eaten him," said Winston. "Those sneaky blaggers. It's a whining shame."

"I don't know, maybe he's still out there," Gizmo said.

Everyone turned to look out across the desert toward the mountains.

Remi shuddered. "It's so…primitive. I wish my humans had moved me to a more civilized environment"

"So do we."

"We'll never see any of them again."

Simba whined. "We're probably going to be next. Heennnngg."

Gizmo stared at the horizon. "Wait. What's that? Out near the sandwash."

They strained to see past the thin bushes and scraggly desert trees.

"Well, Bob's me uncle." Winston danced a little jig. "It's Taser."

"It is!"

Everyone saw him stumbling slowly along the trail. He seemed confused or weary, stopping every few steps to catch his breath, and then continuing on toward the park.

The pack barked madly at the sight of their lost alpha.

Woof woof!

Arf arf!

Bow wow wow!

Yip yip yip!

The weary Lab reached the big drainage pipe on the desert side and started through. When he emerged at the other end in the park, everyone was waiting there to greet him. He collapsed on the grass at their feet.

"Hey!" said Winston. He smelled the dusty dog lying on his side.

It wasn't Taser.

A dry tongue hung out the side of his mouth as he panted pathetically.

"Water," Ranger said weakly. "Water."

TWELVE *Monday Afternoon, later*

I sat down at the spot where I left Ranger and tried to think, but my brain didn't seem to work very well. I felt confused and unsure. I thought I'd told Ranger to wait on the trail right there. I didn't know whether to go home or look for him.

I was woozy from all that chewin'. When I started to stand up I almost fell over. Then I puked. There wasn't much comin' up, just pieces of that awful tasting tree branch. It felt good to get it off my stomach, though.

If only I had my water dish, I'd be in good shape.

I looked down the trail, then up to where I'd been. If Ranger wasn't up the trail he must be down the trail. So I started walkin' down. I got to the tree where Ranger spent some time, but he wasn't there. I tried to look off the trail, but I couldn't see too good, it was like my eye's weren't workin' like normal. Everything seemed fuzzy, especially the Scottsdale houses down below. They were all a blur.

I tried to puke again, but nothin' came up.

I wanted some water, so I looked around for Robert. Robert always had water, I knew he would give me some. I started walkin around to find him. Then I came to another trail goin' off another direction. I figured maybe Ranger went there. I started to walk down that trail, then my eyes got really funny, things were movin' sideways and up and down.

"Meatloaf!"

I sat down and called my buddy's name.

"Meatloaf! Get Robert, I need water."

Meatloaf didn't answer so I kept walkin'. Walkin' somewhere. Up, down, sideways, I wasn't sure anymore. I wasn't sure of anything, except that my stomach hurt.

When Robert looked over and saw all the dogs standing at the drain pipe, he ran over to see what was happening. Then he saw Ranger on his side, panting. He bent down and picked him up in his arms and carried him to the nearest house. He grabbed the garden hose and turned it on so Ranger could lap some water from the end.

Next he sprayed some water all over Ranger to cool him down, then let him drink some more.

The dog pack stood close by watching. Finally, Ranger stood and shook. He walked carefully to where everyone was waiting, then he sat on his haunches. His coat was a mess.

"What happened up there?" Winston demanded. "Was Taser with you?"

"He was," Ranger said weakly. "He's still up there."

Simba got right in his face. "You abandoned him?"

Ranger shook his head. "He ran off to talk to some coyote. That's the last I saw of him. I waited, but he never came back. So I started home without him."

"You left my friend!" Meatloaf growled.

"No! No, it's not like that. He abandoned me. I had to get water or die. It was too long since I had any."

Gizmo raised a paw. "Just tell us what happened."

Ranger swallowed. "I went up to find Harley, but I got in a big fight with a coyote. I was winning but then it knocked me off the trail. I landed in a tree and got my collar caught."

"When?"

Ranger thought. "I'm not sure, I don't remember."

"Then Taser found you?"

"He did. It was sometime the next day. I was really stuck. We tried different ways to get free, but finally he chewed the branch in two pieces. It took a long time."

Gizmo looked at Meatloaf. "What do you think about his story?"

96

"I don't know why Taser didn't come home. It sounds funny." He looked at Ranger suspiciously.

"I'm telling you the truth, I'm not a liar. After we got the branch off, I had to show Taser the way out of the gully. We had to go right past a rattlesnake I killed. Then he started acting all goofy and ran off to play with this coyote."

"That doesn't sound like Taser," Simba said.

Remi sniffed. "Please. That ruffian is perfectly capable of frolicking with the wild life. And Taser has a certain history with coyotes, as I remember."

"Shut up Remi," Winston said. "Ranger, you said Taser started acting goofy."

"He did. He called me Bandit. Who's Bandit?"

Winston exchanged worried glances with Gizmo. "Was this after he chewed the branch?"

"Yes. A little later."

"What kind of branch was it? What kind of tree?"

"I don't know, I'm from Los Angeles. We don't have ugly trees like this in LA. Our trees have nice leaves."

"Yes, yes," Winston said. "But I need to know. Look around the park. What kind of tree was it?"

Ranger turned his head to look. "Well, it was kinda like that one. No, it was more like this one. Yes, this one. I recognize the smell." He pointed with his nose at a thin green tree with small yellow flowers.

Winston breathed in sharply. "Cercidium floridum. Green Palo Verde. A deciduous, low-water, desert landscape favorite. Draught tolerate, freeze resistant. But the bark is poisonous."

"Poisonous!" Simba barked loudly.

"I'm afraid so," said Winston, puffing out his Bulldog chest to his professorial mode. "This particular variety is extremely poisonous to small animals. In larger animals it induces a hallucinogenic state."

Gizmo spoke what they all were thinking. "Is Taser going to die?"

"I'm afraid it depends on how much he consumed," Winston said. "But for certain, his reasoning and judgment will be greatly impaired."

"For how long?" demanded Meatloaf.

"That would be difficult to ascertain." Winston looked out past the desert to the tall mountain. "But I would not expect Taser to find his way home tonight. If he ever does."

***

Whoooooooo,Whooooooooo.

Shut your trap, I tell the dumb owl. I'm walkin' in little circles, tryin' to get a feel for my new home.

My cage is bigger than I remembered. I figured they musta made some changes at the pound, because I got a lot more room now. It's quieter, too, except for the occasional owl hootin' that he wants to go home. I know all about that, I want to get out of here, too. I hate this dog pound.

Maybe I'll get out in the morning.

CLANG!

I jump at the sound of steel bars slammin' home. It's probably the guards letting dogs in and out. It must be meal time, but I'm not getting' up because I'm not hungry. If I eat now I'll just puke it all.

I wish they'd turn that little moon out. I want dark when I sleep. And please guards, get those rabbits out of here, I can't sleep with rabbits runnin' by. This place has really gone downhill.

Water would be good about now.

"WOOF WOOF."

I bark for water. I wish the guards would let me have water. I musta done somethin' to make 'em mad. I'm gonna tell Major all about it. Maybe he'll bite one of them, show 'em not to mess with us dogs.

Major is my hero. When I grow up I wanna be like him.

In the meantime, I'm just gonna lay here with my head on this rock and wait. If you wait long enough, stuff changes. Even if things are bad right then, soon they'll get better. The important thing is not to give up. Even if you got a bad home, someday you'll get a better one, even if you have to run away to find one yourself.

But you gotta be careful out there in the human world. There's good humans, sure, but there's bad ones, too. Not everyone thinks you're cute.

I wonder about Simba and Meatloaf and Gizmo. I wonder if they know I'm stuck in the pound. Robert probably doesn't. He doesn't even know I snuck out. It's all Bandit's fault, that sneaky Weimaraner, always tryin' to make me look bad in front of the pack. Even in front of my best buddy. I called him for help.

"MEATLOAF!"

Meatloaf is probably out lookin' for me. I can always count on him. And my Robert.

I hope they come for me, I need help. I'd get up and go myself if I could get out of this cage. It's probably just as well, my feet are tired. My body is tired. My brain is confused. I'm so thirsty. Maybe I'll just wait right here until things get better.

***

Meatloaf was having trouble sleeping even at his favorite spot on the living room rug. He opened his eyes sometime in the middle of the night and stared out in the dark.

After Robert took Ranger home to Shannon, she made a big fuss over him, squealing and hugging Robert and jabbering on for a long time. Meatloaf was a little irritated that he didn't get a hug after listening to all her talking, but he let that pass. It was a weird time right now.

His buddy was missing.

It wasn't the first time Taser had snuck out and disappeared, and that time ended up alright, so maybe this would, too. Harley was another matter.

Every dog at the park heard the twilight howl again, but they was fussing over Ranger and his return to the park at that moment. They just ignored poor Harley's howls.

After Shannon's house, Robert and Meatloaf got in his Jeep and drove around the neighborhood, calling Taser's name. They went on every street, but they didn't go in the desert. He knew Taser was out in the desert somewhere, all because of the new neighbor.

Stupid Ranger.

They went home and watched television after visiting Shannon, but Robert didn't act interested in the TV show. He kept getting up and looking outside. Finally Robert pulled his hiking boots out of the garage and said something about tomorrow before he went to bed.

Meatloaf walked outside and checked that the gate was still propped open. Hopefully Taser would show up yet. But Meatloaf was scared.

He walked to the metal view fence at the back of the yard and looked out in the desert. He wanted to find his friend, but there was nothing he could do. He was just a dumb dog.

Meatloaf opened his heart and hurled his pain at the night.

OOOOOOOOuuuuuuuuuuuuOOOOOOOOOuuuuuuuu.

***

When I woke up it was dark. Really dark, except for the sliver of moon overhead.

I wasn't sure where I was or how long I'd been there. I looked around my spot. I was on the mountainside somewhere. I could see the lights of the Scottsdale city far below, and they weren't blurry. The desert wasn't moving sideways now.

I tried to remember why I wasn't home, and then I heard a howl. I listened closely, it was familiar. Yes, I knew that voice. It was Meatloaf. He was far away, but he was calling me. I struggled to my feet and found the trail, but nothing looked familiar. I wasn't sure which way to go.

I sat down again and waited, lookin' up at the sky, then down on the city. Time passed, I don't know how much, but it was a while. I thought about water, swimming' in it, drinkin, it, spillin' it. Water.

Finally I felt better and got up to try to go home again. But suddenly I fell back, cowering in fear.

A pair of yellow eyes came straight at me out of the black night.

No!

I moved back against the mountain, terrified. I was too weak to fight coyotes. But I had to. I had to fight, weak or not. I bared my teeth and got ready to attack.

"Grrrrrrrrrrrrrrrrrrrrrrrrrrrr."

"Taser! Stop!"

The form sharpened until it was clear.

"Stop fighting," Dominga demanded. "Why are you here?"

"Dominga?" I tried to think. "I don't know what happened, I'm lost."

"You came for your friend."

"That's right." I remembered then. "Yes. I had to rescue Ranger. I had to chew on the tree branch to free him. Where is Maverick?"

"Your friend went home. But you stayed on our mountain."

"I feel funny, everything is floatin'. It coulda been all the chewin' I had to do. It hurt my mouth and my stomach."

Dominga looked at me closely. "The branch, was it like this one?"

I sniffed the tree next to us. "Yeah, like this."

"Bad tree. We call Arbol Loco. Makes animals very sick."

"I know my stomach hurt a lot after I ate it. But I feel better now."

"You must go home and rest."

I looked around for home, then remembered something. "Meatloaf howled like he was calling to me."

"Yes," she nodded, her concerned face soft in the weak light. "I heard the fat one's call. That is why I search for you." She turned around. "Taser. Follow me. I will take you home."

She started walking down the trail.

101

I followed a few steps behind, not looking at anything but the trail and her thin outline directly ahead of me. She moved quickly through the night, only pausing to look back at me every now and then.

I started to feel better as I walked. My stomachache was gone but I was still thirsty. We walked down the slope and moved toward the lights of our houses. I didn't think, I just walked, trusting Dominga to lead the way and watch for danger.

It seemed like a long way. I wanted to rest my sore pads, but I didn't want to look weak. The coyotes thought all dogs were weak, and compared to them we were. So I kept my mouth shut and kept movin'.

Finally we made it to the grass park drainage pipe. Dominga stopped at the entrance to wait for me. "You can find your den now?"

"Yes. Thank you for helpin' me."

"Remember this. Ikal and Seti will come on the no-moon night."

"Your sons, that's right."

She didn't say anymore, she just turned and ran into the night.

I went through the pipe into the park, glad to be out of the desert and in friendlier surroundings. I trotted across our park grass, found my street and slowed to a walk. When I reached our house, I slipped through the open gate. I was never happier than when I stepped through our dog door.

The first thing I did was go right to my water dish and drink half the bowl. Meatloaf musta heard me slurpin', because suddenly he was right at my side.

"Taser! Where you been? You're making me crazy, dawg. I oughta bite you!"

I looked up at him, water drippin' out my jowls. "I missed you too, buddy. It's good to be home."

THIRTEEN   *Tuesday Morning*

Robert came downstairs early, not even dressed. He found me sleepin' on the floor, or at least pretending to. He just stood there with his hands on his hips, lookin' at me. I thought I was in big trouble so I kept my ears down and my chin glued to the floor. I couldn't stop my tail from waggin', though. My tail seems to have a mind of its own.

But then he got down on the carpet and gave me a hug and a belly rub, then he went back upstairs. I think he gave up on fixin' me. Maybe he was getting used to me breakin' the dog rules. Meatloaf just looked away and shook his head.

When Robert came down again, he was dressed for work. He fed us but I could only eat a few bites. I did drink extra water, though. I told Meatloaf most of what happened on the mountain, but I couldn't remember it all. Parts of the day and night were fuzzy.

Meatloaf said Ranger got home ok, and that he was home resting. That sounded good to me, restin' was all I wanted to do. I didn't get off the carpet all day.

When I wasn't sleepin' I was thinkin' about Ranger. Meat couldn't understand why I wanted to help the obnoxious new guy. But my friend has never been thrown in the dog pound with no friends or anyone to help you. Meatloaf never had a best friend die because he didn't stand his ground and fight even though he was scared. My German Shepherd friend, Major, said everyone is scared sometimes. But even when you're scared you gotta do what's right. And what's right for me is helpin' other dogs when they need it. Obnoxious or not.

I fell into a deep sleep.

I slept a long time, even longer than Meatloaf. By the time I woke up, it was almost time for Robert to come home from work. I finally got up to drink, then went outside to pee and get some sun on my coat. I felt almost normal, I was even hungry for my dinner.

I lay on my back on the grass and twisted around because it felt so good. Sometimes I'm happy just to be a dog. If only I could relax and be a good pooch like Meatloaf, I'd be happier. But I can't. I'm always tryin' to make sure everything's ok. Which reminded me, I still had a missin' neighbor dog.

I asked if there was any news about Harley.

"Yeah," Meatloaf said. "I heard him howl last night. But that was the same time Ranger walked in from the desert, so nobody noticed."

I didn't say anything. I didn't want to let anyone know I wasn't givin' up my search. I didn't tell Meatloaf about Dominga's sons comin' by at no-moon time. Which reminded me of somethin' else, I needed to watch for them. I wasn't sure when it was no-moon time.

"Hey Meat. When does the moon go away?"

"Go away?"

"Yeah. You know, when the moon gets real skinny, then it goes away, then comes back and gets fatter and rounder and then it's really light out at night."

"I dunno."

I couldn't believe that. "You never noticed the moon getting' bigger?"

He yawned. "I don't look at the moon because I don't howl at the moon. That's what coyotes do."

"I'm not talkin' about howlin', I'm askin' when it gets dark at night."

"It gets dark every night," he said.

"No, I mean real dark. Hard-to-find-your-nose dark."

Now he cocked his head. "Why would you want to find your nose in the dark?"

"You never noticed that sometimes it's real dark out and sometimes it's only a little dark?"

He thought. "Nope. I never noticed."

"I need to know about the moon."

"Why?"

"It's important."

"Ask Winston. He knows all the important stuff."

I made a memory to ask our English Bulldog buddy about that. Until then, I'd just hafta check each night.

"How come Winston knows so much?" Meatloaf asked. "He go to obedience school or something?"

"His owners talk a lot. And they're retired so they watch a lot of television."

Meatloaf exhaled loudly. "I wish I knew more stuff."

"Meat, don't be down on yourself. You used to know more stuff, but the second-hand marijuana smoke messed you up."

"I guess."

"I'm glad Robert doesn't smoke," I said.

"I wish I could help you about the moon." He thought a minute. "Maybe you should ask Ranger."

"Why him?" I asked. "Because he thinks he knows everything?"

"No. Because he's coming over tonight."

This was news to me. "Ranger's comin' over? Why?"

"When we were over there, I heard Shannon tell Robert she was gonna bring something over for dinner tonight. She and Ranger are coming over for dinner, to thank us for helping find her dog."

I didn't like that at all. "Oh great." I didn't want to spend any more time with Ranger than I had to. I got my fill of the idiot on the mountain. Catcrap. I jumped up and walked around the backyard. Meatloaf followed me.

"What's wrong?" he asked.

"I don't like Ranger."

"I don't like him either. Then why'd you save his butt from the coyotes?"

"It was the right thing to do."

"So now what?" Meatloaf asked.

"We get punished for me helping. Because now if Robert and Shannon mate with each other, we'll hafta put up with Ranger all the time. We'll hafta live with him."

"No way, dawg. I'm not living with that big mouth mutt. I'll go back to Fresno first."

"Meat, come on, you're not moving away. You'd miss me." I gave him a friendly push with my butt. "Let me ask ya. Is it more important that Robert is happy or that you and me are happy?"

He didn't hesitate. "You and me."

"No," I said sternly. "If Robert's not happy, we're not happy."

"Says who?"

"It's a dog rule."

Meatloaf got up and walked around. "This is your problem, Taser. You got all these rules and codes and honorable things you think you need to do. Don't you ever just go with the flow? Take it a day at a time?"

I shrugged my shoulders. Which isn't easy. "I guess not."

Meatloaf seemed frustrated with me. "You had to save Ranger and now you have to save Harley."

"Yeah, we gotta save Harley. First we gotta find him."

He looked down his snout at me. "I knew it. You're not through getting in trouble, are you?"

I hated to upset my best friend, but I didn't want to lie to him either. "Not yet."

He sighed. "So. I suppose you got a plan."

"Yep."

"You gonna tell me about it?"

"Not yet."

FOURTEEN *Tuesday Night*

Robert was home at the normal time, give or take somethin'. Dogs can't tell real time, but we got a very good idea when it's close to mealtime.

The Animal Channel says dogs have an internal clock, they called it a brain pacemaker, and it controls everything we do. Which is why I don't worry so much when I do bad stuff, I figure my brain is tellin' me what to do. So I do it. You wanna yell at somethin', yell at my brain, not me.

Robert came in and fed us right away, probably because he didn't want Ranger tryin' to eat our food when he came over. Then he went upstairs and we heard the water runnin'.

Meatloaf looked up the stairs toward Robert's room. "Wow. This must be a real date if he's in the water shower."

"I don't hear any franxinatra music."

"Maybe later."

"You think she could be the one?"

"Shannon's the perfect mate," Meatloaf said. "Except for her dog."

"What are we gonna do?"

I had no idea. "We just gotta be tough, Meat. Let's wait and see how the evening goes."

We didn't have to wait long.

I was lookin' out the front picture window when I saw them walkin' over to our house, then we heard the door bell ring. That always triggers our danger warning, we can't help it.

"Woof! Woof!"

"Bow Wow Wow!"

I don't know why we barked, we knew who it was and knew there was no danger at the door. Maybe we were excited. Sometimes I think our mouth has a mind of its own, just like our tail.

Robert smiled and opened the front door wide.

Come in.

Shannon came in carrying a big white dish. Ranger walked in right behind her just bringin' his attitude. He stayed in the entry with us while the humans went in the kitchen with the food.

I nodded, playin' it cool. "Wassup, dog."

Meatloaf didn't say anything to him.

Ranger acted glad to see us. "Hey, guys." He was panting and wagging his tail, acting real friendly. I wasn't sure whether to trust him or not.

"Say Phaser," he said. "I want to thank you for saving my skin up on the mountain."

"It's Taser, but hey, no problem about the rescue. You'd do the same for me, I'm sure."

Meatloaf looked like he didn't believe that. He didn't say anything, he just looked in the other direction.

"I have to tell you something, though," I said. "I don't remember much of what happened. I remember chewin' through that branch, then I got sick, and then next thing I know I'm off the mountain and back in our neighborhood."

Ranger's head jerked up at that. "Really? You don't remember talking with me down in the gully?"

I shook my muzzle. "Hardly anything."

"No? Do you remember me killing that snake when we were walking out?"

I thought back. "I remember there was somethin' about a snake, yeah."

Ranger nodded. "I was telling you all about where I lived in Los Angeles and my dog show ribbons."

"I guess. I'm foggy on all that. You can tell us again later." I really didn't want to hear it, but he was a guest. "Let's go outside."

We ran out the dog door to the back. The first thing Ranger did was lift his leg on one of our patio posts, which really made me mad. I didn't want him markin' his territory in my backyard, so I went over to the post and peed on the same spot myself.

Just to make things clear.

Meatloaf sat on his butt and watched us. He still hadn't said anythin' yet.

Ranger wandered around the backyard, sniffin' everything. When he was satisfied, he came over and lay on the patio with us.

He looked around, then asked us, "Wait. You don't have a swimming pool? Are you guys poor?"

"Nah. We don't need a swimmin' pool. Robert gives us a bath with the garden hose. Who needs a pool? "

"I do. We got a big pool over at my place. Guys, I don't want to brag but I can swim! Honest to dog, I can swim like a champ! The vet told my owner that my feet are webbed between the toes and that's why I can swim so good."

I looked over at Meatloaf. "Uh, Ranger, I hate to break it to you but all Labs can swim."

"Get out of here." He got all indignant on me, like he didn't know. "All Labs do not swim."

"I don't swim," Meatloaf said.

Ranger said, "See, there you go."

I disagreed. "Meatloaf doesn't *want* to swim, because he doesn't like the chlorine smell in swimming pools."

"Why not?

"It's bad for you," Meatloaf said. "Like fluoride."

I didn't want to get Meatloaf started, so I jumped in with some facts. "Ranger, Labs have webbed feet, because originally we're from Newfoundland, and they bred us to set fishing nets off the fishing boats…"

"That's crazy talk. It's obvious I'm a special dog, just look at you two. You're basic black, but I'm Chocolate!"

It was gonna be a long evening.

I wasn't sure how to play it, whether to tease him or ignore him. I'd never me a weirder mutt. I thought Meatloaf had issues with stuff like specism, but Ranger was another level. Maybe he wasn't a purebred, maybe there was some strange bloodline in him. He reminded me of a dog I knew in the pound, Mad Marmaduke. That dog was plain nutty.

Ranger looked around the back yard a little more. "Don't get me wrong, this ain't a bad home, but I like our backyard better because we got more privacy." He pointed his nose at our view fence. The problem with this kinda place is anybody can walk around back and look in your rear windows."

"The view goes both ways," I said. "We don't hafta stare at a block fence, we can see the wild desert right there."

"Yeah, but snakes and critters can come in."

Meatloaf sniffed. "I thought you killed snakes for entertainment. Or was that coyotes?"

"Coyotes, snakes, whatever—they don't bother me, I can handle them. Don't mess with the Danger Ranger, that's what I tell predators. I remember one time in LA when I was lost in this bad neighborhood, and these two Dobermans had me backed up to the wall..."

Ranger talked on for a while about his daring exploits in Los Angeles until Meatloaf got up, hunched his back and took this huge poop right behind Ranger. I mean huge.

Ranger turned around as the rank smell invaded our nose.

"Whoa! Buddy! You need to see the Vet or something. What in doggie-hell you been eating?"

"Could be garbage," Meatloaf said. "Or it might be time for the twice-baked rabbit."

"What? You ate a rabbit?"

"No, I didn't. But I think the coyote that left its poop at the park ate one."

That was such a disgusting picture we got up and moved far-out on the grass to get away from the smell. That's when we heard the twilight howl.

Oooooooooooooooooooooooooooooooooo.

Ranger jerked his head around at the sound. "Hey, you guys hear that? See, it's coming from the mountain, just like I said."

"That's an echo, Ranger. That howl is comin' from inside our neighborhood."

"No way, it's coming from up there. If I hadn't got into a fight with a coyote and fallen off the trail, I would have found Harley by now."

"Coyote fight? I don't know anything about—"

Oooooooooooooooooooooooooooooooooo.

"We got to do something about that poor mutt," Ranger said.

Meatloaf looked at me. "Taser's got a plan. He's gonna save Harley."

"That's great!" Ranger said. "What do you need me to do?"

I was afraid he might want to help, but the cat was out of the bag, or at least the pooch plan was. "Uh, look. The rescue is still in the planning stages. I gotta wait until it gets dark on no-moon day, anyway."

"Why, do you need a bath?" Ranger asked.

"What's that got to do with it?"

"I get a bath twice a month, on the full moon day and the new moon day. That's how Shannon remembers."

I looked his coat over and thought it looked squeaky clean to me. "So when do you get your next bath?"

"Well, I got a bath today because today's the new moon, so I guess in another two weeks I get another."

"Today. And new moon means no moon?"

"Yeah, that's when it's darkest outside."

Meatloaf looked confused. "It's dark when there's a new moon? How can it be dark with a moon?"

"New moon means it just showed up."

"From where? Where did the old moon go?"

"Don't ask me," Ranger said. "I'm a dog, not a scientist."

Meatloaf cocked his head. "What's a scientist?"

111

"It's a really smart human who coulda been a doctor but doesn't like people. So they make them work all alone in a room staring at white machines. I saw it on the Discovery Channel."

"I don't understand these names," I said. "It should be a no-moon, not new-moon."

"I know, but it's one of those human word things. It doesn't make any sense, but they been saying it so long it's too much trouble to change it."

So, I thought. It's tonight. Ikal and his brother were comin' sooner than I expected. That meant I had to sneak out again, and that was pushin' my luck. I hoped I had the strength to do it. I stretched and thought of a plan. There was only one big problem.

I needed to get rid of Ranger before then.

Our guest was already on to the next discovery, somethin' he spotted layin' on the other side of the patio. "Hey look at that! A squeaky-bone! I had one of those when I was a puppy." Ranger jumped up, ran over and pulled a well-worn chew toy out from underneath a patio chair. He came back and sat down with it clamped his teeth.

SQUEAK SQUEAK SQUEAK

Meatloaf was not happy about that. "Hey, Danger Ranger, that's my squeaky bone you're abusing."

SQUEAK SQUEAK SQUEAK

Meatloaf looked over at me with sad eyes. "Can Ranger go home now?"

I checked inside through the glass door. Shannon and Robert were laughing about somethin', it looked like things were goin' good. They each held a beer bottle and were sittin' together on the couch, but not too close. Then I saw her touch him on the arm.

Maybe she was...nope, tennis shoes tonight. But I wasn't worried. I knew it took humans longer to mate. As far as female humans go, Shannon seemed nice enough, and Robert acted real friendly. He looked happy she came over for dinner, so I was happy.

"What are they eatin' in there?" Meatloaf asked. "Does it look like a leftover night?"

I looked closely. "Right now they're eatin' corn chips and drinkin' beer. I can't smell what's in the dish."

"Chicken enchiladas," said Ranger, looking up. "I helped Shannon make them." Then he went back to the chew toy.

SQUEAK SQUEAK SQUEAK

I was right about one thing.

It was a long night.

FIFTEEN   *Two years previous, nighttime…*

Harley was curled up on the passenger seat of the black BMW car next to Doctor Bill. He wasn't scared, just curious about where he was going. It had been a very strange day and night. He was a little sad about Tim-Bop, he sensed his master was hurt and he did his best to help him. But the fact was, Harley never got his dinner and wanted some water to drink. That seemed to be more important right then. A dog's got special priorities, separate from his master's. With the master he had right then, Harley knew he was not very important. He got care but never felt love.

Tim-Bop was not a bad master, but his friend Squiggy was mean. He would yell at Harley and he sensed he was saying bad things. He did not sense any care from Squiggy at all. He never hit the Harley, because one time when he raised a hand to strike him, Harley growled and bared his teeth. Somehow Harley knew that scared humans, and he'd used it whenever he needed to his advantage. But the truth was, Harley didn't like fighting or biting. He was a good dog. He just looked big and bad and black and mean.

Harley glanced over at Doctor Bill driving the car. He seemed like a nice man, he'd even given him cookies. Maybe there was hope for getting a meal soon with Doctor Bill.

The car pulled into the parking lot of a big store and stopped. Harley raised his head in anticipation. He smelled food.

Wait here, Harley, I'll be back.

Doctor Bill got out of the car and walked to where the lights in the building windows were big and bright and people were moving around behind the glass.

This was very different from the world Harley was in before. Squiggy and Tim-Bop used to take him to dark houses where people

114

sat around and talked. These places were dirty and old, not like this new store with bright lights and happy people.

With Tim-Bop, sometimes there would be loud music, sometimes there would be yelling, but never was there love. Sometimes there would be female humans and funny smells and money paper, sometimes not. Sometimes there would be fights.

They would move around at night in Squiggy's old car. Harley sat in the back seat and watched. Once or twice he'd been in the car when those guns made loud noises and people yelled. After that he'd heard the wailing sirens. Sometimes they were stopped with the cars with the flashing lights. Po-lice, Squiggy called them. He said po-lice were bad.

But it was po-lice that came and helped Harley and Tim-Bop. It was po-lice who took Harley to Doctor Bill.

In a few minutes Doctor Bill walked back to the car with a big paper bag. Harley watched him walk over, hopeful is was something for him for dinner.

The car door opened and Harley smelled there was food for him in the bag. His stubby tail whipped back and forth as they drove out of the parking lot and onto a big road with lots of cars.

Very soon they turned down a street filled with houses with bright windows. Bright colored lights hung from many house fronts. Doctor Bill rolled down a window and Harley smelled cooking food and children and many other dogs.

"WOOF!"

He surprised himself with that bark, he figured he must be excited. He couldn't remember feeling this way in a long time. He was excited and hopeful.

The BMW slowed, then swung up the driveway of a big house. They waited as a big door opened and then the car drove in the house. Doctor Bill grabbed the bag and opened the car door for Harley and they went both inside.

Harley sniffed everything. He loved the leather couch and the fresh paint and the pantry doors with food smells behind them, but there was something he barely knew, a house smell that was clean and fresh and happy.

Doctor Bill set the paper bag on a shiny black countertop and removed two big steel bowls and a bag of dog food. He filled one bowl with water and set it in front of Harley and watched while he drank almost all of it. Then Doctor Bill refilled it and put it by the back glass door. He filled the other bowl with food and put it down.

Harley ate it all, his tail stump wagging the whole time.

Is that good?

Harley burped.

Let's go outside.

Doctor Bill opened the back door and they went out. Harley immediately ran to the fence where he smelled other dogs. He sniffed deep and processed what he found.

There was two dogs. They smelled friendly, clean—two males, not much poop smell. His neighbor dogs were of the same breed—Labradors, maybe. Harley wanted to say hello.

"WOOF. WOOF."

Doctor Bill laughed.

Welcome to your new home, Harley.

Harley lifted his leg on the fence and peed to stake his claim.

SIXTEEN *Late Tuesday night*

Shannon and Ranger left sometime after dinner. Finally. I was happy to get rid of them, it was tiring acting polite all evening. Even with a Labrador temperament.

Robert went upstairs to bed and Meatloaf was asleep in the living room. I was out on the patio. Except for an owl, it was dead quiet in our backyard where I sat starin' into the darkness.

Whooooooooo,Whooooooooo.

Whooooooooo,Whooooooooo.

The Screech Owl in our tallest Mesquite tree told me others were still awake, too. It was late, I shoulda been asleep, but I'd slept almost the whole day so I wasn't tired. I told Meat I was sleepin' outside so he'd leave me alone. This was somethin' I needed to do by myself.

My eyes slowly adjusted to the darkness. I could see far out past the bushes to the tree line along the sandwash. I figured they'd show up somewhere close to that spot if they were comin' tonight. Yeah, it was late, but that's when it was safe for them to roam and hunt.

Humans and most dogs didn't like coyotes, but I did. I admired their independence. They didn't need to please their master to get their food, they hunted their own. Not that it was easy to do. They were tough, and that was worth a lot to me.

Time passed, but I stayed there watchin' and finally I saw a coyote pop out of the wash and trot straight toward my fence. Then another came out and followed right behind, single file. I got up and walked to our metal fence to greet them.

I nodded at them as they looked me over, very close and unafraid. I recognized Ikal from the mountain. I was glad I didn't forget that part.

Ikal spoke first. "This is Seti, my brother."

They were the same size and coloring, it was obvious they were brothers. They both had the same tilt of the head as they looked at me.

117

Seti didn't say anything for a minute, then asked, "Taser. You are well now?"

"Yes, better, thanks." I wasn't back to normal, but it would have to do. "You came to show me the howling dog's house?"

"Yes. Can you go to the tunnel?"

I figured they meant the drainage pipe into the pipe. It was the only way to get in our neighborhood that wasn't fenced. "Yes, at the park. I'll run down there now."

They turned and left. I ran to the side gate and jumped at the latch and flipped it up with my nose. I got it on the first try. Then I took off on a fast trot to the park. They were waiting on the grass, just past the drain pipe. They stood close together, one lookin' right, one lookin' left. Then they walked up and met me in the middle of the park.

"Follow us close," Ikal said. "Hide when we hide."

I nodded and we took off down a street. It wasn't my street, but I'd been on it before on walks with Robert. We moved past all the dark houses, walkin' right down the middle of the street like we owned the road. They moved quickly, a fast trot, always lookin' around for threats. I felt tough, like I was one of the coyote pack out on a hunt. For a time, I guess that's what I was.

Every once in a while a dog would bark fiercely from inside a fenced yard, but it didn't seem to bother the two coyotes at all. They probably knew the dogs were locked up tight. I figured they were lookin' for human threats.

Ahead we saw car headlights flash, so they went to the side and we all stood close to a house until the car drove by. We crouched down and blended into house wall. No one would notice us from the car, even if they were lookin'. When the car lights passed we moved back to the road and kept going.

They didn't talk so I didn't say anythin' either. They weren't sociable at all, they were all business. I kept my mouth shut and dogged their heels all the way across our neighborhood.

118

It was so late most all the lights in houses were out. The no-moon night helped hide us from anyone who might be up.

Finally we came to a street I'd never walked down before. It was at the far end of our group of homes and next to the shopping stores. These houses were older and smaller than ours. A lot of them looked empty. Their yards were dirty, one house had a broken window, another had some spray-painted words on the garage door. The trees in the yard looked more like the trees in the desert with their low-hanging branches. They hadn't been trimmed or cleaned for a long time.

I guessed these were what Gizmo saw, the houses that were abandoned from the economy.

Ikal stopped in the middle of the street next to a house with dead grass. He looked at Seti, then at me. "Taser. This it is. This is the place of bad smells, your friend is here."

I looked at the house where his snout pointed, and I sniffed. I got a strange but very powerful hit. I'd never smelled anythin' like it.

"Harley's here? Are you sure?"

"From here, three howls at dark time."

"Yes, that's it. That's him."

Ikal looked at me like I was weak. "What will you do here? You are but one small dog against humans."

I didn't know what to tell him. He probably didn't know why I was there. "I need to look around, make sure Harley's inside. Maybe I can figures out how to save him."

The coyote brothers just looked at each other.

I didn't blame them for doubting me, it looked impossible. But I didn't want them to get in trouble over dog problems, they had enough of their own.

"I can do it alone, you can leave now. Thank you, and thank Dominga."

Seti stepped close to me. "Taser. Be careful at this bad place. We sense much danger."

119

That stunned me for a minute. I was still thinkin' about that when they ran off, leavin' me all alone. I waited, hearing dogs barkin' here and there as they moved through the neighborhood toward the park and their path home. Suddenly I didn't feel tough or brave. It was all on me now.

I walked closer, up to the front of the house so I could see in the windows. I got up on my hind legs and put my front paws on the window edge and looked in. I couldn't see anythin', someone had put dark cardboard or paper on the glass. I moved to the next window and tried to see in, but it was covered up the same.

Next I checked the big garage door, sniffing at the bottom for clues. There was more of that strange smell but it was stronger. Maybe they had somethin' stored in the garage. Something stank.

For a minute I had the thought it could be a body, maybe someone died there. But it didn't smell like that, I knew what dead smelled like, because one time a dog died in the pound close to my cage. You never forget that smell.

If it wasn't death, what was it about this place that scared Seti and Ikal? I needed to find out.

I moved to the side yard and the fence gate. The fence itself was strong cement block, but the gate was made of wood slats on a metal frame. I pushed on it. The gate was locked, but some of the wood slats hung free. I nosed the loose ones out of the way and thought I might be able to squeeze in.

I got my head inside but my body was too tight. For a minute I wished I was as thin as a coyote. They would get through the broken gate easy. My ribs were stuck, so I breathed out all my air and pushed through. The slats swung closed behind me. I had to be careful, escaping wouldn't be easy.

Now I was standin' in the side yard. I could see the backyard was in even worse shape than the front. One tree was dead and half-fallen over. Broken cardboard boxes were layin' here and there, along with old trash, mostly beer bottles and old food boxes. I saw two big empty barrels. It stunk like garbage, but that other smell was there, too.

There were huge electric wires comin' out of the bottom of the wall and goin' up to the electric box. I'd seen electric wires before and I knew what they could do, so I kept my distance. And these wires didn't right, they hanging were out in the open. Maybe that was the danger the coyotes sensed.

I crept along the side of the house, searchin' for a dog door or a window I might be able to see in. I couldn't find one, all the windows were covered up. Then I got a smell of somethin' else, somethin' that I hoped to find when I got in there.

Harley's smell.

There was no sign of a dog in the side yard. No dish, nothin' chewed, no poop there.

So I sneaked carefully all the way to the back yard. I slowed, listening, sniffing. The smell of Harley was strong there. I moved to the rear, padding slowly, then I just peeked around the corner of the house and saw what lay on the patio.

Oh No!

***

Meatloaf woke up and stretched, then looked for his buddy at his normal spot on the living room carpet. Taser wasn't there.

That's right, he's sleeping out back.

Meatloaf yawned and stretched. He got off the floor and hit the dog door to pee on the outside bush. While he was peeing, he noticed the side gate was open.

Now what?

He walked to the gate and looked out front, then walked to the back to check Taser's dog house. It was Taser's dog house because Meatloaf refused to go in it. He knew that plastic was bad for you so he certainly wasn't gonna breathe plastic fumes while he slept. He didn't want to get cancer or have any six-legged puppies. His master in Fresno told him all about it.

What was the stuff called again? Thermopolyuncarbonated or something dangerous-sounding like that. He didn't like that humans had nice-smelling houses and dogs got hermopolyuncarbonated plastic houses.

It was specism.

His human in Fresno explained all that stuff to him, but now it was confusing to Meatloaf. Still, he wouldn't eat plastic so why would he sleep in it? Meatloaf would eat anything but he wouldn't eat plastic, so it had to be bad.

It was bad enough that they poisoned everyone by putting fluoride in the drinking water.

Meatloaf looked around some more, but Taser wasn't sleeping in the doghouse, in fact he wasn't anywhere in the backyard at all. He sat down to think. Why would Taser leave again? He tried to remember. Maybe he did say something about looking for Harley.

That's right, on the no-moon night. Meatloaf looked up at the sky, searching. No moon. Taser was probably out looking. He should have taken some help, Meatloaf would have gone with him. Even with his limp he could still be valuable.

Meatloaf thought. Taser better get home before Robert wakes up. He's in enough trouble already, he doesn't need any more.

And they think I'm the dumb one.

***

Taser peered around the corner at the sad sight.

His friend Harley was layin' on his side on the concrete patio. He had a thick collar on that was attached to a heavy metal chain running to the concrete post. He certainly looked dead. I walked closer, sniffing. Then I called his name, quietly.

"Harley."

122

He didn't move. I looked at his chest, it was moving up and down as he breathed. Finally I could exhale.

"Harley. Wake up."

His head jerked up and he opened his eyes wide. He blinked twice, like he was dreamin'. "Taser? That you?"

"It's me. What are you doin' here?"

"I'm inna heap a trouble, Jack."

"Why! What happened to you?"

"You hear my howls?"

"Yes, everyone heard them. We heard you when we were at the park. That was smart, Harley. The pack figured out you were talkin' to them."

He put his head back down. "I ain't so smart, lookit me now. I be all messed up."

"Why are you chained up here? Who did this to you?"

"Bad humans. Be careful they don't get you, Jack."

I looked him over. He wasn't cut or bruised but his coat was a mess, just like the bare concrete patio we were on. Dog poop littered the patio all around us.

"Do they feed you?"

"When they think about it. Which ain't often. The only water I gets is old and stinks."

I turned around and looked at the house. This was a bad situation. "These humans. Are they sleepin' in there now?"

"Dunno, probably not. They come and go, moving stuff in and moving stuff out. They gots me chained up here for their watch dog."

"Watch dog?"

"They think I'm a mean Rottweiler. They don' know I'm a big cupcake."

I shook my muzzle. "You shoulda stayed home."

"Tell me about it. But I snuck out, I was tryin to get some sugar. This dog needs a little sugar now an' then. I knew it would get me in trouble someday. This be it."

"How'd you get caught?"

"I was walking down the street and they drove by, stopped and offered me a hamburger. Then they stuck me in the back of the car and took me here. They bad dudes, Jack." He exhaled a pathetic sigh. "I wanna go home, Taser. Please help me. I miss Doctor Bill."

"Don't worry, we're gonna get you outta here." I looked at his heavy chain. Catcrap. There was no way I could chew through metal. I looked at the dark house.

"What are the humans doin' in there?"

"I don't know. When the back door opens up, I see 'em in there working on stuff. They got buckets of plants inside."

"Plants?"

"House plants, you know. Little Palm trees"

"Is that what smells funny?"

"Yeah. And they gots all these lights on. It seem like the lights be on inside for two days, then they off for a day, then they come on for two days. It's weird, I tell ya. Crazy place."

I knew this was bad. We were in trouble. "Harley, I may need to come back with help. This chain…" My voice trailed off. I didn't want to discourage him, but it looked impossible to save him.

"Taser, please. They leavin' in a day or two. I heard 'em talkin, they be leavin' here soon and takin' me with 'em. If you don' get me quick, I ain't ever comin' back."

Now I was really worried. I tried not to show it. "Harley, don't worry. I won't let them take you."

"I'm in a heap a trouble, Jack."

I looked around the back yard for clues, anything. I saw a lot of weeds, an old rusted bicycle, a broken wheelbarrow but not much else. On the other side of the house back fence was the shopping stores parking lot. There were no clues, and nothin' I could see that would help Harley escape here. We would have to bring our own tools. Or a human, somehow.

I tried to comfort him. "You can count on our pack, buddy."

SLAM!

I jumped up when I heard a door slam. Somebody was in the house. I heard humans talkin' to each other in loud voices, but I couldn't understand any words.

Harley's eyes got huge and round. "Taser! Run. They back!"

"Harley, I'll come back for you, I promise."

"Run!"

I ran.

I ran to the broken gate, pushed the loose slats to one side and started through. But I caught my coat on somethin' and couldn't move. It was my ribs, my ribs wouldn't go through the slats. All of a sudden I heard voices out on the patio. The humans were outside.

"WOOF WOOF!"

Harley barked, warnin' me to get away.

Then I remembered, I had to breathe out all my air—only then I could slip through the gate. When I got my ribs free I crept up front and peeked at the visitors. There was a car in the driveway with a human sittin' in it.

A human came out of the house and went to the car trunk. He took a box out of it and carried it back in the house. The motor was runnin' on the car but it wasn't movin'. It was a newer car, but it was dirty, too.

I lay back down and tried to melt into the ground like I saw the coyotes do. I waited, the human in the car didn't move. I couldn't see if there was anyone else, but I didn't want to wait any longer.

I crept forward a little at a time, then waited, then crept some more. Finally I slipped to the next-door neighbor's house. I lay there a minute, then I hit the street and ran like a scalded dog. I finally stopped at the end of the road, shakin' from the fear of what could have happened. I stood and panted, tryin' to calm myself down.

You're OK, Taser.

Yeah.

125

I was free but Harley was still chained up. I trotted home, tryin' to come up with a rescue plan on the way. I had to think of a way us dogs could break that chain.

SEVENTEEN *Wednesday Morning*

I was exhausted. I'd barely slept at all after I got home because I was tryin' to figure out how I was gonna help Harley. I told Meatloaf about it as soon as he woke up.

"That is crazy, dawg. Poor Harley. What are we gonna do?"

I didn't know. "We have to get ideas from the pack tonight."

"And television," Meatloaf said. "Remember that Dizzy channel movie about the cat and the two dogs lost in the mountains? They had to cross rivers and mountains and they got home ok."

"Yeah, but this is more like that Dalmatian movie, the one where all the puppies get kidnapped by those crooks."

"And the weird skinny lady," Meatloaf said.

"What was her name?"

"I dunno. The only one I remember was the fat puppy who was always hungry."

"How'd they get away from the bad guys? Do you remember?"

"The neighborhood dogs rescued them."

"Yeah, but how?" I asked.

"Does it matter? That was a movie. This is real life."

Meat was right about that. And in real life dogs don't chew through a metal chain locked to a concrete post.

"Let's ask Winston tonight," he said.

"Oh." I almost forgot something important. "There is one more thing, Meat."

He eyed me suspiciously. "There's always one more thing with you. What is it?"

"The humans are packin' up and movin' soon, and they're takin' Harley with them. We only got a day to get a plan and rescue our friend."

127

Meatloaf sat on his butt. "That's great. Anything else you didn't tell me?"

I thought. "Did I tell you about the lights inside the house?"

"No. What about them?"

"They got lights inside that come on for a couple days, then go off."

"That's weird."

"And the whole place has a funny smell. Harley said it's the plants."

Meatloaf cocked his head. "Really. These plants, are they inside or outside the house?"

"Inside. Harley saw them when they opened the door. But the odor is everywhere. I don't think humans could smell it, but us dogs and the coyotes did."

"What's it smell like?"

"It was new to me. I don't know what it was."

Meatloaf thought. "You ever been sprayed by a skunk, or smelled a dead one laying in the street?"

I'd never been sprayed by a skunk, but I heard it was a bad thing from other dogs. "Nope. I don't think there's any skunks in Scottsdale. I know there aren't any in Westside Phoenix."

"The marijuana smell, it's kinda like skunk. I bet the smell at the house is marijuana plants."

"Why would you think that?"

"My human in Fresno used to grow his own marijuana in one of the bedrooms. He wouldn't let me go in there, but one day he left the door open and I could see he had lights shining on the marijuana plants."

"Did he have dark paper over the windows?"

"Aluminum foil, he didn't want anyone looking in. He was always worried about the feds, what ever that is. He was a little strange, but a good human. He always shared his bag of potato chips with me. Sometimes we'd eat a whole big bag while we were watching cartoons together."

I didn't know much about marijuana, and probably wasn't gonna have time to learn before we had to rescue Harley. Besides, I don't think Robert got the Marijuana Channel.

"So what now?" Meatloaf asked.

"We wait for the park tonight. Maybe the dogs have more answers than me."

***

When twilight finally came I was ready for help. Nothing Meatloaf or I thought of would work to cut the chain. I hated to admit defeat, but it wasn't about me, it was about saving Harley. At park time waited by the front door, then ran ahead of Robert all the way from the house to meet our friends before they left.

I went right over to Winston and Gizmo, even before I peed. I wanted to get the story out before Ranger showed up.

"Guys, big news, I found Harley."

"You're kidding."

Winston's head snapped up. "Bloomin' hell?"

"Last night. You know Dominga, and it's a long story, but her sons knew where Harley was."

"How'd you find that out?" Gizmo asked.

I quickly told them about most of it, I figured they should know if they were gonna help.

"Wow. Marijuana."

Winston agreed with Meatloaf's guess about what the plants were. "*Cannabis Sativa,* of course. It all makes sense, now. Taser, you've been a busy lad. But what can we do about it? At times like this, I wish we could communicate with out masters."

Gizmo got right to the point. "We've got to save him. What's your plan, Taser?"

They all looked at me. I was the alpha, I should have the plan—but I didn't. "Look, I gotta admit I'm stumped. You guys got any ideas?"

"Well," Winston said. "We need to be aware of what we're up against, and I think these humans are a formidable lot."

"Why?" Meatloaf asked. "They're just harmless potheads."

Winston disagreed. "I think not. I believe these are hardened criminals. Growing marijuana is big business."

Meatloaf scoffed. "My owner grew it in Fresno and he wasn't a criminal. He only grew medical marijuana."

"Personal use is one thing, but this sounds like a pot factory. There are a lot of distressed rentals with this economy. Criminals are renting these vacant homes and filling them with hydroponics cannabis farms. They can make millions with a few grow houses.

"Millions?" Gizmo shook his head. "No way."

"It's true," Professor Winston said. "A house the size of ours could have a hundred plants, with three growing cycles a year, that's almost a million dollars a year. Indoor pot brings more money, because it is higher quality."

"That's crazy," I said.

"The point is," Winston insisted, "with that much money at stake, these humans will be dangerous. They may be killers."

"Yes, yes. But Harley said they were leavin' soon and takin' him away. We gotta act tonight."

"Tonight!"

"I'm sorry but we're out of time."

"We need a plan," Gizmo said. "Taser, you got no idea what we can do?"

I was ashamed to admit I didn't. "I'm sorry, guys."

"Sorry about what?"

It was Ranger walkin' up. He was the last dog I wanted to see right then.

"We need a rescue plan," Roxie told him. "Taser knows where Harley is."

"Excellent. Where is he?"

Winston told Ranger the whole story. I looked at Meatloaf and rolled my eyes. I'd hoped we might avoid including our obnoxious neighbor in our plan.

Ranger listened intently, then interrupted. "Marijuana. I know all about that, I'm from LA."

"That's nice," I said. "But we're tryin' to figure out an escape plan. We can't chew through Harley's chain. It's heavy metal."

"Really?" Meatloaf's eyes widened. "I know all about Heavy Metal. My Fresno human was a head-banger."

Ranger ignored him. "What's the chain attached to?"

"It's wrapped around a concrete patio post and locked tight."

"Locked? With a metal lock?"

"Yeah. The chain goes all the way around the post and is attached with a combination lock."

"You'd think potheads wouldn't be able to remember the combination numbers," Meatloaf said.

Winston objected to that. "These are not potheads, these are professionals. Serious criminals after serious profits. That makes this a serious business."

"And we're in serious trouble," I said. "We're out of time."

"I have a plan," Ranger said.

I was afraid of that. "Ranger, really…"

"Let's hear it," Gizmo said.

Ranger stepped forward. "A chain is only as strong as its weakest link."

I looked at him impatiently. "That's your plan?"

Gizmo held up his paw. "Let's hear him out."

Ranger went on. "I wasn't there, but I can see Harley chained to the post in my brain. I can see the solution."

"Tell us."

He dragged it out, enjoying the moment. "What's the weakest link in Harley's chain?"

"The lock?"

131

"The post?"

"No," Ranger said. "It's the other end. It's Harley's collar. All we gotta do is get his collar off and he's free."

"That's brilliant," Roxie said. "Humans can do it, so we know collars come off."

"But how can we do that? Dog collars are made so dogs can't figure it out."

I knew that was true. And you can't get your mouth under it to chew. "Ranger, when I tried to get you free of that branch, I looked at your collar. It's got this complicated latch."

Everyone thought a minute.

"I got it," Winston finally said. "We need to fight these hardened criminals with a hardened criminal. We need a bloody safe cracker. We need Spike."

"Of course."

"Who's Spike?" Ranger asked

"He's the Doberman who lives a couple streets over. His owner lives here in a Federal Witness Protection program. They used to be in the mob back east."

"Spike could crack a collar," Gizmo said. "But I don't know if he'd come with us. He's awful grouchy these days."

"When are we going over there?" Ranger asked.

"We go tonight," I said. Everyone needs to meet here at the park tonight. Gizmo, can you flip the gate latch for these guys?"

"No problem." He looked around. "Who's all coming?"

It looked like it was me and Meatloaf, Winston and Roxie, Ranger and Gizmo.

I warned them about identification. "Make sure everybody has their collar with tag tonight. There's a chance we may get caught and end up at the dog pound. If you want to get home you need your license tag."

"Good advice. What time do we go?" Gizmo asked.

That was a problem, we had to coordinate.

"How about this," Gizmo said. "I'll come by after my human goes to sleep. Listen for me. I'll bark three times at your gate, that will be the signal for everyone. It will be late, after the funny guy on television is over."

"Which one?"

"The letter man."

"He's not funny."

"Either way, it's a good plan," I said. "We'll go to see Spike, then go to Harley's. It's dark with the no-moon so we should be alright."

I looked at Ranger. "Hey, dog. Great plan. Thanks for comin' up with such a good idea. You really helped us out."

Ranger beamed.

It was about dark now and our humans were getting' ready to leave. I turned my ear up to the night. "Hey pack, it's past twilight and I haven't heard Harley howl."

"You're right."

"That's not good."

Everyone looked at each other, probably thinking the same thought. Maybe they'd left with Harley already. Maybe we were too late.

Roxie hung her head.

Heennnggg, Heennnggg, Heennnggg.

EIGHTEEN *Wednesday Night, around midnight*

It was very dark and very quiet. We lay outside, close to the gate, waiting for Gizmo. Meatloaf was sleepin', or as he claimed, conserving his energy.

I put my head on my paws but I was afraid to go to sleep myself, I didn't want to miss the hyper Jack Russell. I felt a little funny askin' all the dogs to help, I didn't want anyone to get in trouble or to get hurt. I was beginning to realize our attempt could be dangerous.

I got up and took some runs at our gate latch, I wanted to be ready to leave when Gizmo showed up. It took me three tries, I musta been nervous. When the gate opened I sat down and waited.

Pretty soon I heard Gizmo bark across the street at Ranger's fence. I poked my head out and looked, Roxie was with him. He leaped to the top of Shannon's fence and into their back yard. In a minute he had the gate open.

"Meat. Wake up, it's time to go!"

He got up yawning but moved quickly with me out to the street to meet the group. Everyone was there but Winston.

"We can get him on the way to Spike's house," Gizmo explained. "They live close to each other."

"Which way?" asked Ranger.

"Follow me and no talking." Gizmo took off at a fast trot with us in tow. He passed five houses and then turned at a cross street. I checked over my shoulder at Meatloaf, he was limpin' but not too bad. I wasn't sure if he should be goin' with us, but he acted like he really wanted to help.

Gizmo turned down the second street and ran to a single-story house with a bunch of cactus in the front yard. He barked three times, but not loud enough to wake up humans.

Winston's squat form appeared at the gate. Gizmo hopped over and soon Winston was pantin' in our face.

"Alright lads, the time has come for us to save the day. The game is afoot!"

And off we ran. A pack of six mutts who knew they were the last hope of a brother in trouble.

***

Harley rolled to the other side and tried to get comfortable. His shoulders and hips were sore from lying on the hard concrete patio. Finally he sat up, dragging his heavy chain as he rose. He looked out in the darkness, wondering if Taser was ever coming back, and if there was anything he could do if he did.

He didn't want to tell Taser how mean these humans were, so he'd kept quiet about his bruised ribs. From then on, he'd kept out of the tall humans way. The fat human was nicer, he was the only one who fed Harley, even if it wasn't often enough.

Harley's stomach growled, he needed food right now. He couldn't remember how long it had been since he ate.

He got up and walked back and forth on the patio, dragging his chain with him to one side, then back to the other. It was his only exercise. He was tired, but he forced himself to keep doing it. He needed to stay strong. If sometime the humans made a mistake and let him off the chain, he wanted to be strong enough to bite and run.

So he walked. Left ten steps, right ten steps, left ten steps, right ten steps. Every now and then he would pull the chain tight and push away, flexing his powerful muscles against the immovable force holding him back. His toenails scraped the patio as he strained, the heavy leather collar digging deep into his neck.

Then he'd rest, panting.

They were starting to pack up their stuff, they'd taken most of the plants. For a minute Harley didn't know what would be worse, the

135

men abandoning him there, chained to die in the back yard, or taking him with them.

At least if they took him, he would live to have another chance to escape. It would be better than dying here alone. All he could hope for was his friends to come save him before it was too late. If only they would.

Harley hung his head, overcome with sadness. He cried out for someone, anyone to help him.

Ooooooooooooooooooooooooooooooooooooooooo.

***

We all stopped in our tracks at the sound of the plaintiff howl.

"Bloody hell."

"It's Harley, he's desperate."

I turned to the pack. "We gotta hurry."

We took off runnin' the last two houses to Spike's place. We assembled in front of the fence gate, standin' close to Gizmo as he barked quietly but urgently.

Woof-woof, woof-woof.

We waited, then Gizmo barked again.

Woof-woof, woof-woof.

We heard the dog door slam and suddenly saw a black Doberman snout and two glowing eyes.

"What's this?" Spike growled. "Some sorta shakedown?"

Winston knew him best, so we let him talk.

"Spike. Terribly sorry to disturb you at this dreadful hour, but a friend of ours has fallen into capture and we intend to release him. We hoped you might help us out."

Spike's eyes narrowed when he spotted me standin' in the pack. "Blackie. I should known you were involved wit dis. And here's Meatball, even." He looked at my buddy.

Meatloaf didn't answer him.

136

Next Spike looked over at Ranger. "I don't know dis brown dog."

Ranger stepped forward. "I'm a Chocolate Lab!"

Spike looked him over. "I'm happy for ya." He looked back at me. "Dis is about Harley, right? You're lookin for da Rottweiler. I told ya all I know."

I nodded. "Yes, but now we know which house he's at. I was in the backyard and talked to him."

"Dat right? So whadda ya need me for?"

"We need your help cracking his collar," Winston said. "We thought your breaking and entering skills might come in handy."

Spike considered the challenge. "Collar, eh? Yeah, I can open collars. But I get a lot of bones for dat, usually."

"We can bring you bones, can't we, dogs?" Winston looked at us.

Everyone nodded.

"Yep."

"Sure."

"No problem."

"Dat's good, 'cause collars are tricky," Spike said. They got this one flap that tucks deep into da buckle. Ya gotta get dat out, then pull and flip da little set pin at the same time. It takes a sensitive mouth. Youse guys are lucky I'm available."

"Yes, yes. So you'll come with us?"

"Why not. I could use a little excitement. This burg is as boring as a Jersey City bar on Sunday mornin'."

"You think you can open it?"

Spike puffed out his chest. "No problem. I remember one time we were after this champion greyhound, a big winner, and he had 'dis extra-secure collar, but it was real thin so… Uhh, never mind about that, let's go."

"Gizmo can flip the gate latch to get you out."

Spike smirked at that. "Dat right. Well I don't need Gizmo ta flip anything, I got my own way out. Meet me on da other side of my house."

We hustled across the front yard. When we got there Spike emerged from a hole under the fence behind a bougainvillea bush. He shook some dirt off his graying coat.

"I like ta keep my options open," he said. You never know when the cops might raid the place. So I keep dis hole available." He looked in the direction of Harley's captive house. "Dat way, right."

"Right. Let's go."

Now there were seven of us. We walked single file on the sidewalk with me leading the way. We moved quickly, with a sense of urgency but now with fresh hope. If Spike could get the collar off it would all be worth the risk.

I stopped countin' streets and relied on my innate sense of direction. Somehow I knew exactly where I was goin'. It was like Harley was sending out a homin' signal and it was floatin' right into my brain.

Suddenly I saw car headlights flash ahead.

I turned to the pack. "Hide!"

I ran to the closest house and crouched close to the wall like I'd seen the coyotes do. Everyone followed. The car drove by, slowed, then turned down a street out of the neighborhood. I stood up.

"Close call."

The pack stood up.

"That was fun!" Ranger exclaimed a bit too-loudly.

I counted noses before moving on. Someone was missing.

"Where's Spike?" I asked.

Spike stepped out of the shadows where he'd made himself invisible. He looked at Ranger with disgust. "Fun? What is dis, amateur hour? Taser, send 'dis guy home, I ain't workin' wit no amateurs."

Ranger acted insulted. "Hey, I'm no amateur. You want to send somebody home, send Meatloaf. He's got gas something terrible."

I knew that myself. "Look, Meat's got something bad goin' on in there, he says he ate something weird. It will pass."

Ranger scoffed. "That's what I'm afraid of. I'm not walkin' behind him anymore."

"Alright, break it up," I said. "We're all goin'. Come on."

Meatloaf shot Ranger a dirty look but let him go ahead of him.

We walked until we got to the last street in the subdivision. I started down the sidewalk, checkin' left and right. Everyone followed until I stopped three houses away and pointed my nose. "It's just over there."

Spike stepped forward. "Blackie. Let's you an' me case this place. We'll come back and get da amateurs if it's all clear."

"Right. But we need Gizmo," I said. "He's our special forces dog. He can do anything."

"Fine." Spike turned to the pack. "Da rest of youse guys wait in the shadows. Be sure and bark if anyone comes."

We left them and moved quietly to the house. Gizmo and I let Spike lead the way. He moved silently along the front of the neighboring house, poppin' in and out of the dark shadows. He stopped when we got to Harley's house. We crouched down and talked in low tones.

"What's da story?" Spike asked.

"Harley's chained on the back patio. The gate's locked, but we can slip through the loose slats. It's tight, but you can make it."

Spike nodded. "The house looks empty, but let's check it."

"The humans come and go. They got a bunch of marijuana plants in there."

"Yeah. I smell it. Looks like a grow house. I hear dere's a lot a bones in weed. Alright. Let's go in da back and check it out."

He took off before I could answer. When we reached the fence I showed him how to flip the slats to one side so he could slip through. He was so thin it was no problem for him. He went first, then Gizmo, then I squeezed through.

We stood in the rear sideyard and looked around. I saw the covered windows were brighter than the last time I was there. "The lights are on inside."

Spike nodded.

Gizmo noticed the electrical wires coming out of the wall. "Look at that. Be careful of those, remember what I told you. These wires look powerful."

"Right."

I led the way to the corner of the house, stepping around broken glass bottles and new trash piles. "Harley," I called quietly. I hoped to warn him of our presence before he barked.

A chain rustled on the patio. We stepped around the corner and saw Harley standing there.

"Spike! Gizmo!" he said. "This is great."

"Quiet. You ok?"

"Yeah, but how are we…"

"Spike is here to work on your collar. He says he can get it off."

"I hope so."

Spike moved forward and examined the heavy metal chain on the ground, the padlock, and finally the collar around Harley's neck. "Beefy. Two inch leather. Metal grommets. Double set pins."

He shot me a look, I didn't know if it was good news or bad.

"Alright, lay down."

Harley started to lay down.

"No." Spike said. "Other side."

Harley flipped over on the other side and put his head down. Spike bit at the strap and pulled. It didn't budge, so he tried again. Then he looked up. "Dis may take a while. Tell them dogs out front to stay out of sight."

"Ok," I said. "Gizmo. You stay here in case Spike needs anything. I'll tell the guys."

"Right."

I ran to the gate and pushed through after exhaling. The wood scraped my side so much I thought I may be cut from it. I jogged down two houses where the pack was waiting. They all milled around me, anxious for news.

Roxie bounced in anticipation. "Is Harley there? Is he alright?"

140

"He's fine. Spike's workin' on getting' the collar off. He says you guys should stay here out of sight."

"Fine by me." Winston looked relieved.

"Ok." Meatloaf looked tired.

"But I thought…ok, I guess." Roxie looked disappointed.

"No way," said Ranger. "I want to help you guys."

I didn't need a mutiny at this point. "Ranger, we need you here. We need someone to watch for the criminals. If they show up, you gotta warn us before they find out what we're up to."

He brightened at his assignment. "You can count on the Danger Ranger."

"Good." I ran back to the house, then walked to a front window and looked, just in case I could see anyone. It seemed deserted, but I was quiet. Then I went around back to the rear patio. Spike was still workin' away on the collar.

"Any luck?"

"He's got the first strap out," Gizmo said. "He's working on the hard part now."

I paced back and forth, waitin' on Spike. Every now and then I went to the gate, stuck my head through to make sure everything was alright. Then I heard my name called.

"Taser!"

It was Spike. I ran to the back to see what the matter was.

"What's wrong?"

Spike looked up from his work. "We got a problem heah. Dis model collar—". He shook his head. "It's a tough one. I may have bit off more than I can chew."

Harley raised his head and looked into my eyes. Right then I decided I wasn't leavin' there without him.

"What's the problem?" I asked Spike.

"I can pull da strap, but I can't flip double set pins at da same time. Dis model is super secure."

I moved closer and looked at it. He needed help. He needed two mouths. "Maybe I can bite the pins while you pull the strap."

Spike shook his head. "Not enough room for two of us down there." He stared at the clasp, then looked up. "Not wit your muzzle anyway. Who's the smallest dog we got?"

I knew what he was thinkin'. "Roxie."

"Get her."

I looked at my friend. "Gizmo. Run get Roxie, tell her we need her help."

"Arf!" Gizmo jumped up like someone stepped on his tail.

I tried to keep Harley's spirits up. "Don't worry buddy, we'll get you out."

He didn't answer, but he didn't look like he believed me. He just lay there breathing quietly. Spike gave me one of those worried looks again. Then suddenly Roxie was there at Harley's side, talkin' gently to him, her little tail waggin' like crazy.

"Hey, you big lug. What the heck are you doing here?"

"Roxie!"

Spike jumped in. "We ain't got time for dis. You. Roxie. Ya see dose pins?"

"Yeah."

"When I pull on da strap, da pins comes loose. But you gotta flip 'em out and hold 'em while I let go a da strap. Got it?"

"Got it."

"Let's try it."

They went to work while Gizmo and I walked to one side to talk.

"How's it look?' he asked.

"I dunno. If I had to bet, I'd say it looks bad."

"What's happening out front?"

"The pack's watchin' for humans."

Just then I heard a commotion at the side yard, somebody grunting and groanin'. Gizmo and I ran over.

It was Ranger stuck in the gate between the slats.

142

"Help," he said. "I'm stuck."

"Ranger, you idiot, what are you doin'? You're supposed to be watchin' out front."

Ranger panted as he strained to free himself. "I got bored. I wanted to help. Oww!"

I looked closer. He was stuck tight, his ribs were jammed into the wood slats on either side.

"Breathe out," I told him. "Push out all the air in your lungs."

He tried but it didn't work.

"More air. All of it."

Finally he gave a little yelp but got free. He stepped through and shook himself. "Wow. That was a tight fit."

His predicament reminded me of a problem with our escape, but Gizmo was already there.

"This opening isn't big enough for Harley to get through," the Jack Russell said.

"You're right." I was starin' at it when all of a sudden Ranger took off for the backyard. "Wait," I called to him as we ran up. "Don't touch these electric wires."

He looked at them. "Why not?"

Gizmo got in his face. "They're hot, dummy. They're bypassing the electric box to run the lights. They're dangerous, they can kill you. Hot wires caused that fire at Taser's, you know." Gizmo glared at him.

"Don't get excited, I got it. Where's Harley?" He ran around the corner and up to where Harley lay.

"Wow," Ranger said to Harley. "You're really in trouble here."

Harley looked at him while they worked on his collar. "Who are you?"

"I'm Ranger. I'm from LA."

Spike stopped workin' and looked right at me. "Get dis mutt outta heah."

"Ranger," I said. "Come with me."

143

Ranger followed me around the side of the house to the gate. I pointed at the opening with my snout. "This needs to be bigger so Harley can get through. You need to chew on the wood on both sides where it's too tight. Make the opening bigger."

"Right."

I left him to work on it. I knew it was gonna take a little time. I ran around back, it turned out they were havin' some good luck and some bad luck with the clasp.

"They got it once," Gizmo said, "but then it slipped back."

I nodded. We didn't say anymore, we just watched Spike and Roxie work. I looked up at the sky, it was blacker than the inside of a dog food bag. That was one thing in our favor.

Spike raised his head. "Gimme a minute ta rest. I'm old. My neck is killin' me."

I was feelin' sorry for Spike when I heard something out in front of the house. It sounded like a car door slam. Then we heard barking.

Woof Woof Woof Woof

It was Meatloaf.

The marijuana humans were home.

NINETEEN

Winston and Meatloaf stood underneath a neighbor's Mesquite tree, watching the street in case any criminal humans arrived. They saw Ranger run to the back gate and get himself stuck halfway through.

Meatloaf shook his head. "I told Taser not to bring that guy."

Winston nodded. "He's a loose cannon."

"Yeah." Meatloaf thought a minute. "What's a loose cannon?"

"Loose cannon on deck." Suddenly Winston sniffed the air. "My word! Is that you?"

Meatloaf looked around. "Sorry. My stomach is really churning. Probably all the excitement. I think it's something I ate at the park."

"Really, dog, you should see an Internist about that."

"It'll pass through eventually, everything does. But tell me. Loose cannon on deck, what's that mean, anyway?"

Winston pontificated. "The sailing vessels of old were constructed of wood, not iron and steel like ships today. English Oak was particularly prized for its strength and beauty. But in a raging storm, sometimes the heavy iron cannons would break loose and roll around the deck, crashing into the cabin or even the tall sail masts. The effect could be as devastating as a volley of cannon balls from marauding pirates."

Winston paused for emphasis. "A loose cannon could very well sink its own ship."

Meatloaf watched the stuck Chocolate Lab. "Yeah. That's Ranger, alright."

Finally they heard Ranger yelp as he squeezed the gate through and passed into the back yard.

Then they went back to watching. A Siamese cat snuck by across the street, but they ignored it. They crouched down as a car drove up the street, but it drove on by without stopping. They kept watching.

145

"I'm tired of this," Meatloaf announced. "They never let me do anything. It's because I limp, isn't it."

"I don't believe that."

"They think I'm stupid."

"Every dog has different gifts. Your's is… Your gifts are…You can…"

"I can catch criminals just like Taser can."

Winston softened. "Of course you can. It's just the fewer in the backyard the better. Ranger shouldn't have gone in there, but he's a stupid blighter. Can't tell him anything.

Meatloaf looked at the backyard. "They get to have all the fun, while we have to watch the house."

"Consider yourself lucky, my boy. They're not having any fun in there, I can assure you. Besides, I doubt you and I could fit through that broken gate if…wait!"

They crouched down again as a tall van drove up to the house, slowed. Then it swung on the driveway.

"Uh oh."

The doors swung open and two men stepped out, one tall, one chubby.

"Catcrap. Now what?" Meatloaf asked

"We've got to slow them down." Winston started to move. "Wait until I get over there, then bark a warning to Taser." Winston ran toward the truck.

Meatloaf waited a minute, then barked loudly.

"Woof Woof Woof Woof"

Winston barreled toward the first human leg he could reach and bit down hard. He clamped himself like a leech, determined to slow them down.

OW!

The fat human danced around with Winston hanging onto his leg in a death grip. He swung awkwardly in a circle, trying to free himself from the Bulldog's jaws. Winston swung in the air as the human cried out.

Hey, get this crazy dog off my leg.

The tall human was laughing so hard he nearly fell over. He pointed at Winston. *Don't worry, that dog will be dead from your blood soon enough.* He laughed even more as he walked to the front door and opened it.

The fat human followed him, dragging Winston along inside the house.

Winston wasn't letting loose.

"Grrrrrrrrrrrrr   Grrrrrrrrrrrrrr   Grrrrrrrrrrrrr"

***

Spike and Roxie were workin' frantically on the collar and I didn't know what to do to help. It looked hopeless.

Suddenly Spike leaped up. "Got it."

Roxie backed away as Harley got to his feet and shook. "You did it!"

I jumped in the middle. "We gotta get out of here now, the humans are out front." I turned and ran toward the gate. "Run!" I called out.

I rounded the corner and saw Ranger squeezing through the slats. *Oh No.* He stopped movin', it looked like he was caught.

I ran up behind him. "Ranger, exhale!"

"I am." He groaned and pushed with his hind legs. "I think I'm swollen from the first scrape."

Now all the dogs were stacked up behind him at the gate, anxious to get out of the backyard.

I tried to coax the stuck Labrador. "Ranger. Breathe out all the air in your lungs. You can do it."

As he exhaled Spike stepped up and bit him on the butt. Ranger yelped but it didn't help him get unstuck. I could hear Meatloaf barking and the humans movin' through the house. Soon it would be too late for us.

I looked at Gizmo, it wasn't too late for him. "Gizmo. You can jump over this fence. Save yourself."

He looked at the fence top, but shook his head. "I'm not leaving my friends."

Hey you!

We turned. A tall human started comin' toward us with this angry look on his face. A fat human limped along behind with our crazy Bull Dog hangin' off his leg.

"Grrrrrrrrrrrrrr, Grrrrrrrrrrrrrrrrrr."

Finally, Winston let go and ran over to stand with the pack, spitting and hacking out pant leg. "Thought I had the blaggard for a moment."

The human looked at us like we were dog poop on his shoes. *What the hell is this? A damn dog party?*

The fat one looked around. *How'd the Rottweiler get loose?*

We huddled together and waited to see what would happen next. Spike wanted to attack them.

"Harley," Spike said. "We can take those two humans."

Harley bared his teeth. "The tall guy is mine."

"Don't try it," Winston said. "That fellow has a revolver in his belt. A .38 Smith and Wesson, I believe. Quite lethal to canines."

Catcrap. There was nothing we could do against a gun.

Jimmy. Block off that gate. We gotta get loaded up.

Whadda we do with these dogs?

When we get loaded, we'll take the Doberman and the Rottweiler with us. We can lock the rest of 'em inside the house and let 'em rot.

I looked around at the friends I'd gotten into this mess. "It looks bad."

Gizmo glared defiantly, his chest muscle rippling. "This ain't over yet." He looked like a coiled spring.

The fat human limped over toward us and the gate. We moved away cautiously, exposing Ranger stuck half in and half out of the gate.

He stared at this new problem, mumbling. *Stupid mutt.*

He grabbed a hold of Ranger's back legs and pulled once, twice. Ranger yelped but popped back in the rear yard with us. He ran over and stood with us. Then the human rolled one of the empty steel drums in front of the gate opening so we couldn't get out.

When that was done he stared at us with disgust until his friend called out.

Jimmy. Come on. Help me load up the last of it.

Jimmy rubbed his leg. *Stupid mutt.* He kicked at Winston but missed as Winston side-stepped his foot. Jimmy turned away and limped slowly into the house, mumbling to himself. *Stupid dogs.*

Gizmo came to my side. "Now what?"

I looked around at the backyard. "I'm thinkin'."

Spike walked over to Ranger and got in his muzzle. "Nice work, Fido. You really screwed da pooch dis time."

Ranger hung his head. "I messed up. I never shoulda…I'm sorry."

I knew all that was true, but fightin' wouldn't help us get out. "Let's go in the back, maybe we can see what they're doin' in there."

"What if we send Gizmo for help?" Winston suggested. "He can raise a racket that would bring humans if not police."

"Not enough time," I said. "Maybe we should all rush them what they open the door."

"Might work. Some of us will get shot, though."

I didn't think so. "I doubt if they'll want the police called over shooting. The problem is gettin' out the front door if we overpower them and get in the house."

We huddled by the back fence, waiting.

Suddenly Ranger starts talkin'. "Guys, look. I need to confess something. I'm not really from LA. I'm just an average dog. I'm nothing special."

Roxie tried to stop him. "Look, Ranger, maybe this isn't the best time."

"Yes, it is," he said. "I wanted to fit in, to be a big shot. I'm sorry I screwed up so bad. Look at the mess I got my new friends in."

149

We let him talk. We weren't goin' anywhere for a while.

"I'm a liar. I never hunted coyotes," Ranger said, hanging his head. "Coyotes scare me. I was running from one when I fell off the mountain. Taser is the brave one, not me."

"Ranger—"

"I'm not a pure bred anything."

"Ranger—"

"I can't blame you guys for hating me."

"We don't hate you—"

The rear door swung open and the tall human came out and messed with the chain and the padlock for a minute, then carried them both in the house, leavin' the rear door open. I could see the inside was almost empty. I knew it wouldn't be long now. They'd take Spike and Harley next.

Suddenly Ranger got up and walked to the side of the house.

"Where's he going?" Gizmo asked.

"Maybe he's got to pee."

Ranger got to the corner and looked over at us, then stepped up to the electric wires. He took one of the fat wires in his mouth and pulled hard.

"No!" Gizmo yelled as he ran over. "Don't touch that!"

Ranger kept jerkin' and pullin' the wire. The lights inside the house blinked once, then again, then shut off. It was dark inside and out.

"Ranger, no!"

He kept jerkin the wire, then all of a sudden I saw a bright flash of light in the house. The human inside stared yellin' somethin' to his friend, and the next thing we smelled was smoke.

Roxie looked scared. "What did he do?"

White smoke drifted outside and then we saw flames inside.

"Oh no." Roxie backed into the far fence corner and crouched down. Heeennnggg. Heeennnggg. Heeennnggg.

150

Smoke really started pourin' out of the back door, it smelled so strong I couldn't smell anything else. I felt the heat on my coat and backed up myself.

We huddled together in the fence corner, as far away from the house as we could get. It wouldn't be long until the heat and smoke would reach us. I didn't want to die there. "We gotta get out the gate, it's our only hope." I looked at Harley. "I bet you can move that barrel."

We ran toward our only exit, then stopped in our tracks. Ranger was layin' by the wires on his side, not movin' a muscle.

Roxie yelled out. "Ranger!"

Spike stepped forward and sniffed his face. He looked at me and shook his head.

Oh, no. We'd lost a brother anyway.

I heard the doors slam on the truck out front, then tires squealing as it raced down the street. The fire was spreading fast in the house and it started to get smoky and hot on our side.

Harley ran past us to the metal drum in front of the gate and put his body against it and pushed. It rocked from side to side. "Spike, help me," he called.

They both got up on their hind legs and pushed. The barrel fell over and they quickly rolled it away with their heads.

I looked at the space. The opening was chewed but it was still not big enough. "We gotta chew the gate open a little more."

Harley put his mouth on the wood and bit and chewed quickly as the fire grew in the house. It was getting bright in the backyard from the flames, brighter then day-light.

I ran back to Ranger and checked him one last time to be sure he was gone. I nudged his limp brown body with my snout, then backed away as the heat got too intense. Sparks floated in the air and singed my coat. I looked at Ranger sadly, then over at the pack huddled by the gate. Smoke poured into the yard and burned my eyes. I coughed and walked over to the group.

We couldn't wait much longer. We had to get out, soon.

Harley backed away from his chewin'. "Let's try it. Roxie, you first."
He nosed the slats away as Roxie jumped through, then Gizmo, then Spike.

"Go," I told Harley.

He stepped through the chewed opening, paused as he rubbed, but cleared the sides with a little scrapin'. I moved up to follow him, lookin' back one last time at Ranger motionless on his side. I let out a sad sigh, then stepped through to the front yard.

I ran to stand with the others watchin' the fire two yards away. The sky above the marijuana house filled with bright yellow sparks. We could hear sirens warblin' far off in the distance.

It wouldn't be long until the fire humans arrived, maybe it was time to leave. I started to say somethin' to the pack, then I looked left and right.

"Hey. Where the heck is Meatloaf?"

TWENTY

It was dark in the back of the van.

Meatloaf hunched down behind the tall stack of marijuana plants, hiding the best he could from the two humans in the front seat. He'd made up his mind when he saw them loading up the van that he wasn't gonna let the criminals get away. He'd show Taser that he wasn't the only dog who could save the neighborhood.

Meatloaf slipped in the side door when they went inside for another armful. He felt pretty clever as he settled in for the trip. He wasn't sure where they were going, but he'd deal with that when they got there.

The two criminals drove quickly out of the neighborhood toward Phoenix.

That was close.

What the hell happened in there?

It's Charlie's crappy wiring. I told 'em it was shoddy work.

Now what? They're gonna be pissed.

Then let 'em hire a union electrician next time.

Fat chance of that.

Let's just take this load in and get something to eat. How's that leg?

It hurts. Damn dog.

Don't sweat it, those dogs are all barbeque meat by now.

Meatloaf listened closely, he was very excited but very nervous. He was so nervous his stomach cramped. That was understandable; he wasn't used to capturing criminals. Nor was he sure how to actually do it.

No worries.

He figured an idea would come to him.

Eventually.

***

"Meatloaf!"

We did a quick search around the area, thinking maybe that Meatloaf hid somewhere when he saw the fire in the house.

"Meatloaf!"

Everyone called his name.

"Meatloaf!"

When we couldn't find him and he didn't answer, we re-assembled in a pack a couple house away, then looked back at the marijuana house. The fire was well underway. Yellow flames were dancin' from a hole in the roof. I listened, the wailing sirens sounded very close.

"Now what do we do?"

"First Ranger dies and now Meatloaf disappears."

"This is bad."

Spike looked nervous. "Look, dat's all a shame, but we better blow dis joint before cops show up. I ain't takin' no rap for a house fire. I'm too old for hard time."

I knew Spike was right, but I couldn't leave without Meatloaf. "Gizmo. Take these guys home, make sure everyone gets there alright."

Gizmo hesitated, but agreed. "Ok, yeah, we should get home." He hesitated. "Look, I'm sorry about Ranger, but he…" His voiced trailed off.

They all trotted off down the street. I watched them go, saddened about our new neighbor's death but now worried about my buddy. I hid under a bush and waited in case Meatloaf appeared.

A long fire engine showed up first. A bunch of guys jumped out and ran around connecting hoses and sprayin' water at the house. If I hadn't been so worried I woulda enjoyed all the craziness.

A radio cackled as a police car showed up and two police-humans got out with lights flashin'. I ducked even lower so they wouldn't see me.

At some point a fire human came out front carryin' a very limp Ranger, so limp it looked like all his bones were gone. He set Ranger down by the curb and covered him all up with a white cloth. Then he went back to workin' on the fire. It was then I felt really bad about all this. I knew Shannon would too.

I kept waitin' and watchin', but Meatloaf never appeared. I figured he musta gone on home, so I decided to go home myself. It looked like the fire-humans had everything under control. I turned and ran down the street, there was nothin' more I could do.

Besides, it would be gettin' light soon and wanted to get home and check on Meat. That crazy pooch, it was always hard to tell what he was gonna do. He probably didn't even know himself.

***

It wasn't very long before Meatloaf knew he'd made a big mistake.

He thought they were still close to the neighborhood because they'd only been driving a few minutes. He didn't have a plan yet, but that wasn't his immediate concern. He really had to go. He should have taken care of business before he got in the truck, but he got caught up in the moment.

Now his stomach was cramping and he couldn't wait very much longer. He knew it must have been that coyote poop. He made a memory not to do that again. Just because it smells good, didn't mean it's smart to eat it.

But that wasn't helping him at the moment. They were driving on the big road with a lot of cars and trucks. He thought he recognized the sign of the big home store, so he hoped maybe they'd stop and Mack and Donald's house and maybe he could sneak out. He needed a potty break.

Suddenly Meatloaf couldn't hold it anymore. His back hunched as wet poop exploded out of his rear in a fury that scared him.

PBBBBBBBBBBBBBBBTT.

155

The poop bomb plastered the marijuana plants and sprayed all over the wall of the van. Then it came again.

PBBBBBBBBBBBBBBBTT.

The sound reached the human's ears first.

What the hell was that?

Don't look at me.

Then the smell invaded the front of the truck.

Ahhhhhhhhhh!

The tall human driving slammed on the brakes and the van slid sideways off the road. Two men frantically rolled down their windows and stuck their heads out, desperate for some fresh air.

The driver parked the van half-on the road in his haste to get out of the truck. Cars coming up behind it swerved around, honking angrily. The fat passenger and the tall driver through open the doors and ran ten feet away from the van. They stood on the road shoulder and looked at their truck in disbelief.

What the hell is that smell!

I swear, the fat human said. *It wasn't me.*

Meatloaf sat in the van patiently, waiting. Let me out please. This may not be over.

Go open the side door and air it out.

Yeah, please.

I'm not going near that truck.

It was at that moment that Meatloaf heard a car motor and saw flashing lights directly behind the van. The lights strobed inside the truck windows, alternately displaying and then hiding the results of Meatloaf's extreme gastric disaster.

Two Scottsdale Police officers got out of their car and walked up to the van. They shined their flashlights in the face of criminal number one and then criminal number two standing off to the side.

What's the problem here, gentlemen?

Ahh, no problem, officer.

Why is your car parked halfway on the highway?

156

I... We had an unfortunate medical emergency.
What's wrong?
My friend here had some sort of intestinal problem.
I told ya, it wasn't me.
Could I see some identification?

They fumbled in their pockets as the second officer sniffed the air, stepped closer and then jumped back. He pointed at the van and spoke sharply to the two men

Just a minute. Would you open your vehicle, please.

The driver glanced downward. *Sorry officer, no can do.*

Sir. I asked you to open this door.

Officer, I know my rights. You got no probable cause here.

Yes, we do. I know what death smells like, and something in that van is dead.

Something *is* dead in here, Meatloaf thought. It's a rabbit that got in this van the hard way.

***

Sunrise came and went without Meatloaf. By the time daylight arrived I had convinced myself he'd run in the marijuana house tryin' to save us and got burned up in the fire. That meant his license tag got burned up, which means no one would ever be able to tell Robert, because they wouldn't know where he lived.

It seemed we saved one dog but lost another. Maybe we lost two dogs, if Meatloaf actually died in the fire. It was not my best week. I didn't want to think about it. I put my head on my paws and sighed deep. It was bad enough losing Ranger.

I thought it would make me feel better if I talked to Harley, so I went outside to the back fence. I stood at his corner of the yard and barked for him.

"Woof, Woof."

I heard some scuffling and rattlin' on the patio and then Harley filled my nose.

157

He called over to me. "That you Taser?"

"Yeah, how are you feelin'?"

"I feel great, I gots me a huge bowl of food and lots a lovin'. My master was so happy to see me. Can't thank you enough, Jack."

It was good to have the big dog home. Now if only…

I told him what happened. "You know, Meatloaf is missin'. I don't know where he is, I hope he's alright."

"That's crazy. What happened to the bro?"

"Beats me. Let's hope he turns up. I'll talk at ya later, Harley."

"It's cool."

I walked slowly back in the house, dreading the rest of the day. I dropped my belly on the tile and soaked up the cool temperature. All I could do was wait.

Heenngg, Heenngg, Heenngg

And whine.

It was almost time for Robert to come downstairs and get the news papers when I heard the doorbell ring. I ran to the front window, looked out and saw a black and white Scottsdale police car parked right out front.

Catcrap.

They must have seen us dogs at the marijuana house fire. I could hardly believe they'd caught me so quick. I didn't bark when the policeman rang the bell because it's a dog rule—don't bark at cops unless you want to go to the slammer.

When no one answered he rang once more.

Finally Robert came down the stairs and opened the front door. I stood right behind him. We both saw a police officer standing there with a tired Black Labrador on a short leash. My tail started whippin' back and forth crazy at the sight of my buddy.

Robert smiled, too.

Good morning, officer. What have you got there?

Meatloaf came in the door all casual-like and plopped his flabby body down on the living room carpet while the police-human spoke to Robert.

I was nearly barkless. "Meat! Where you been?"

"Sorry I'm late," Meatloaf said. "I was busy catching criminals." He walked over to his favorite spot on the rug and plopped down. Suddenly a panicked look crossed his face as he stuck his nose in the air and sniffed frantically.

"Hey! I didn't miss breakfast, did I?"

EPILOGUE *Four weeks later, late at night*

I was stretched out like I was asleep, but my eyes were open. The house was so quiet it woke me up. My bones ached a little because I was sleepin' on the tile floor and suffering for it. The tile floor is cooler but a lot harder than the carpet.

The day had gone fine. Too fine, I guess. I was bored. I resisted the urge to walk over and chew one of the dining room table legs. So I lay there a while, rememberin' things that had happened in the time since Ranger and the house fire and Harley returned.

Everything had settled down in our little neighborhood. Nobody moved out and nobody else moved in. The money economy wasn't any better and there were still too many ugly heads on television, but us pack dogs were happy.

The latest news was Harley's doctor-human married a female, a nurse female. Meatloaf said that's why females go to nursing school, so they can get out, mate with doctors and move to Scottsdale.

Either way, this new female got Harley trained somehow not to bite. Meatloaf said Harley musta gone to anger-management school. Whatever it was worked good, because now Harley comes to the park with us after dinner. That was great news for Roxie. Every once in a while she and Harley disappear in the bushes. I knew what was goin' on in there, but I didn't say nothin'. Humans don't need to know everything.

One good thing happened. Robert doesn't complain about money or bills anymore. It could be the govament gave him some Chinese money, I'm not sure. Meatloaf thinks he's getting extra money at work, because he dresses better than he used to. Now he wears a suit coat every day with his shiny shoes.

It seemed like Shannon got over her loss of Ranger ok, because she got another dog, a puppy this time. She probably wanted to train it from young to act better. That hasn't worked for her yet. She brought the little guy over to our house last week when she and Robert had dinner. The first thing it did was pee on the rug, right where Meatloaf sleeps. That's normal puppy stuff.

It's a Yellow Lab.

I got mixed feelin's about that, but I'm prejudiced. Get black or go back, I say.

Meatloaf is real happy because he got a lot of attention for catchin' the marijuana criminals. He even got his name in the news papers. Robert clipped out the section and taped it on the kitchen wall down by Meatloaf's bowl so he can see how famous he is. Ever since then, Winston calls him Sheriff Joe, Arizona's toughest Labrador.

I'd argue with that, but hey.

Even Spike is friendlier to us now. He doesn't come to our nightly pack party, but he and his master walk by now and then. It turned out that Spike wouldn't take any of our bones for freeing Harley. He said the collar crack was on the house, whatever that means. I think he's startin' to trust us dogs after he saw us helpin' one of our own.

I sighed. The quiet all over the house was makin' me jumpy.

I rolled on my other side where I wasn't flat and settled in again, twitchin' my paws and sighin'. Outside, I heard that Screech Owl again.

Hoooooooo, Hooooooooo.

It was hopeless, I knew I couldn't get back to sleep, so I got up and went out our dog door. It was warm, so I knew the hot times were comin' and soon me and Meat would be inside layin' under the airconditioning more.

I walked to the back fence and looked out in the desert, remembering how hard the hot-time was on the coyotes. I hoped they could get through it alright. I hadn't heard much of them lately, but I knew they were around because I could smell 'em. Every now and then I picked out Dominga's howl from the other desert voices.

Like that owl.

Hoooooooo, Hooooooooo.

Suddenly I sniffed deep, sensing a new presence out in the desert. I stared through the fence, trying to see what it was.

After a while my eyes adjusted to the dark and I saw two sets of yellow eyes far out by the sandwash. The eyes stared at me as I stared back. Finally they swung away and walked off in the dark.

Somehow, I knew the coyotes would be fine.

End

The following is the first chapter excerpt from:

A Howl in the Night

A Howl in the Night is also available as an audiobook now!

ONE

As soon as I heard it, I knew something was terribly wrong.

It was long, low, and mournful, like a little hound heart was broken and nothing would ever make it right. A thousand hairs on my back stood straight up. Even Meatloaf woke up, and nothing wakes him up.

He thought it was the wind whistling through our wood-slat gate. It was the hot time, and sometimes dust storms blow in out of nowhere, like tonight. But I knew this was a different animal altogether.

I cocked my head like some mutts do when they don't get it, except I knew exactly what was up. Just then a big wind gust slammed the house, blowin' a bunch of seed pods out of our Mesquite tree and sending them raining down all over the patio.

That was it.

We bounced off the living room rug and bolted for the backyard. Pow! I blew the dog door at full speed, Meatloaf clippin' my heels. We stopped and went rigid out on the grass, straining to hear through the storm. The wind raised and rustled the long hairs of my black coat. I took a step forward and listened harder, desperate for a clue. Then it came again.

Wooooooooooooooooooooooooooooooooooooooooooooooooooooo.

I shivered, even in the warm breeze.

It was Nelly, the little Beagle three-houses down. I'd heard her howl before, but not like this. Never. That's when I knew somethin' awful must have happened.

We looked helplessly at each other, there was nothing we could do, Nelly was three houses away. That's three yards with tall block fences and wood-slat gates as tight as a chain choke collar at full yank. Meatloaf let loose a couple of mean, rumbling barks, hoping to scare off whatever might be menacing the neighborhood. I did a quick perimeter check, ears up and nose to the ground. I nodded at my partner. The yard was clear.

Harley next door started with his baritone bark, then Roxie down the street, except her squeak wouldn't scare away a mouse. All around the neighborhood, dogs spoke up to warn the unwary—not at my house.

Meatloaf stood by my side. "Whadda ya think?"

I had my nose in the air, searching for tell-tale scents. "I don't like it. Smells like trouble comin' our way."

We ducked as a white light streaked past our house and flashed down the street, then streaked by once again.

Police-humans.

We dashed to the gate and stuck our noses through the slats. Best as I could smell, there was a lone female-cop at Nelly's place. Somebody must have called the police, probably that old busy-body across the street from us. She didn't sleep much, except during the day when we wanted to bark at cats.

Ghhetricmmspdpvkjfresjjttheehhsk.

A two-way cackled with cop talk in the night air, bouncing off the neighbor's house and funneling into our backyard. I knew a lot of human words, but I couldn't make any sense of this babble. No matter, I thought I knew what was up.

"Gotta be a burglary," I said.

Roxie was still barkin' on and off, and of course Harley the Rottweiler wouldn't shut up. Neither would that radio.

Kfjkfhjwurirnchdjdotiwmerhddhh.

We ran to the other side of the yard, but nothin' was shaking so we hustled back to our gate. I was gettin' nervous, the police shoulda been out of there by now. It was startin' to look bad for the Nelly household.

"Here comes another one," said Meatloaf.

There were two more, actually. Now we had three cop cars and two light bars strobing our street. It'd be different if this was Saturday night at the Deuce, but this was Scottsdale, baby. Nothin' bad ever happens up here.

"What about the police?" he asked.

I sniffed deep. "The female's still inside, but now there's four males out beatin' the bushes."

"Don't know, dawg, that's a lot of police for a burglary."

Meat was right. That many cops in one place usually meant a beer bust or a body turning cold. Even in this heat.

Then it hit me. The scent was faint, very faint—then all too strong. It floated over on the thick night-air when the wind died, invading my strongest sense. I stepped to one side and threw up. Meat couldn't smell it, but watching me retch, he knew what made me puke.

Blood.

"Woof Woof! Woof Woof!"

Meatloaf let 'em have it again. That started another round in the neighborhood, so I joined the chorus.

"Bow Wow Wow Wow!"

That felt great—until we got the word from the man.

Taser! Meatloaf! Get in here.

Busted.

Robert held the door open and waited for us. He had that face on. No barking.

Heads hanging, we trudged back inside. I don't know if Robert heard the police but he didn't miss our warning. He told us again to shut it, then he turned out the light and went upstairs. It looked like the block party was over. Pretty soon it was as still and quiet as a pooch on the way to the vet.

167

Meatloaf plopped down on the carpet and went right out. He was snoring in no time, but I couldn't get poor Nelly out of my mind. Her sad howl reminded me of a bad affair and a hapless hound I've tried to forget. I put my chin on my paws and stared out into the darkness, thankful for my master and the roof over our heads.

When sleep finally came, my tired paws twitched and jerked to that same nightmare, that same horror, that same moment.

***

My eyes popped open at first light, but I lay there a while and analyzed the action at Nelly's. I tried to find a good side, but every way I flipped it, it came up trouble. Meatloaf and I know all about trouble, we been around the block before. We didn't just fall off the animal-control wagon.

By the way, we're Labs.

Black Labs.

Meatloaf was still sleeping, but I got up and stretched my legs. It seemed like it was brighter outside, which was a good thing, first-food would be coming up quick. I heard Robert moving around upstairs—heavy footsteps, water splashing, doors closing—stuff like that.

I was gettin' impatient, I wanted the day to get rolling. I'd have gone upstairs to see what the holdup was, but that's a big "No-No, Bad Dog" around here. But it was time to go, even Meatloaf started to stir from his spot on the carpet.

The noise upstairs got louder, so me and Meatloaf moved to the bottom of the stairs to whine and wait. When you're a dog, you spend most of your life waiting. Waiting for food. Waiting for pats. Waiting for a walk. If you're Meatloaf that's no problem, you just plop down and rest. Me, I gotta move.

So I left him huggin' the floor and went to see what was happening out front. I nosed the window shutter open and right away I spotted a rabbit sittin' in the yard. That just made me crazy, but I chilled. Those

168

rabbits sit there like a statue and think we can't see 'em. Spottin's not the problem, catchin's the tough part.

I turned my head and saw a couple black and white cars down the street. At least that's the color I thought they were, because I got dog's eyes, and they stink during the day. According to the Animal Channel, we see shades of grey, washed-out yellows and blues—but no red or green.

A bark rumbled deep in my throat, but I choked it off. I didn't like these cop cars in my neighborhood, but I didn't want to make a fuss before we got something to eat. Sometimes you gotta stay focused.

Hi, guys!

It was Robert. He came down the stairs and rubbed our bellies while we rolled around on the floor like a couple of idiots. Robert went out to get the papers so I followed along to check things out. The rabbit outside was long gone, no surprise to me. The minute you get close to those long-eared rats they disappear like a dropped grape rolling by Meatloaf's nose.

Robert snagged the papers and glanced down the street at the black and whites. I wanted him to go check it out, but he went back inside to feed us, so I didn't wanna complain. I get a little nervous if I don't get my food first-thing, 'cause you never know if they're gonna forget you. Sometimes humans get their priorities screwed up.

So we got a couple cups of dry Eukanuba in separate bowls. I got the performance blend, Meat got the weight-control type. I don't much care for it; neither does my buddy, but he'll eat anything. I scarfed my chow down in a hurry so he couldn't steal any, then we hit the water dish for slurp and burp.

That's when the doorbell rang.

Normally we bark like crazy at the door bell, but I kinda expected this visit so I gave Meatloaf the look. I've seen these black and white cars before. I saw plenty of them during my time on the Westside; they bring cops in dark-gray uniforms with lots of questions. This morning I wanted to hear those questions.

I've learned a lot of human words in my time. It's not that unusual for a dog, not like a mutt opening a door or using a fork. I'm beyond all the normal words—eat, park, treat, stay—every hound knows those and more. Some dogs know a lot more, like me. You just gotta listen, these humans know some stuff.

We sat perfectly still in the living room so Robert wouldn't lock us up in the garage, but I put both ears up when they started talking. I picked out the human words I knew.

Good............Scottsdale.Police............hear............noise......
...killed.......neighbor............call.........anything...

Pretty soon I can't help it myself, I started pacing back and forth and whining.

Heeennnnnggg. Heeennnnnggg. Heeennnnnnnnnnnnnnnnnnggg.

Robert pointed his finger at me.

Taser! Hush!

I needed to tell them about Nelly's howl last night, but they wouldn't listen to me. I don't get why they can't understand my words. I think it's a lip problem, their little human lips open and close real tight when their words come out. Me and Meatloaf, our lips don't close real good, they just kinda hang there, sloppy-like.

The cops finally left. Too bad, we didn't learn squat from that visit, it looked like we had to wait for dogs-at-dusk, our nightly mutt-meeting down at the park. If anyone knows what's goin' down around here, it's the neighborhood dogs.

170

A PG version of Howl in the Night is available as
A HOWL AT MIDNIGHT
For Young Readers

Made in the USA
San Bernardino, CA
16 January 2013